Fary, Princess of Tiali

NAFISSATOU DIALLO

TRANSLATED BY
ANN WOOLLCOMBE
EDITED BY
BARBARA HETZNER SCHERER
DESIGN BY
W. W. WEEMS

FARY
PRINCESS
OF TIALI

©Ann Woollcombe 1987

First English Language Edition
Three Continents Press
1636 Connecticut Avenue NW
Washington, D.C.   20009

ISBN: 0-89410-411-X
　　　　0-89410-412-8
LC No.: 83-50541

Cover art, drawings by Wendy W. Weems
©Three Continents Press 1987

Dedicated posthumously to the author

Table of Contents

Foreword

Fary, Princess of Tiali is a West African Cinderella story about the marriage of Fary, a beautiful, low-caste Senegalese girl, to Prince Bocar, a repugnant, twisted dwarf. The tale takes place in one of the four Wolof states along the Atlantic coast where the caste system was once rigidly observed, and for this reason the marriage is most unusual.

The text contains some French and Wolof words which may be unfamiliar. Fary herself belongs to the *griot* class, the French name for the bards who were members of the second, occupational caste. (The Wolof word for bard is *gewel*.)

Prince Bocar belongs to the highest class, the *jambur*. (A prince is called a *buumi* in Wolof.) The freeborn—noblemen, aristocrats, land-owners, and cultivators—were in the first class.

Artisans shared second-class casted status with *griots* and were the metalworkers, leatherworkers, jewelers, woodworkers, shoemakers, and weavers. (In Wolof, they are *ngenyo*. *Griots* were the lowest of this caste.)

Slaves comprised the third class, with their own class system. The slave of an artisan could not marry the slave of a nobleman, although his master would pay the bride-price if a slave wanted to marry a woman who belonged to someone else.

Membership in all classes was inflexible and fixed by birth.

* * *

Griots occupied an ambiguous position in Wolof society. Although they were intelligent and influential in their role as bard, historian, reporter, and publicity agent, they were also, and sur-prisingly (at least to Westerners), the most scorned of all classes; they did not mix with the ruling nobles or even ordinary commoners.

However, despite their low caste, *griots* were unique in their ability to associate with all classes of Wolof society. They were con-sidered intellectuals on a par with priests, and were valuable teachers whose tales supplemented the knowledge passed on to children by families and clerics. As keepers and narrators of all genealogy and history, they had to know everything about everybody, telling all or withholding a detail here and there, if "the price was right."

In the *griot* group itself, there was a hierarchy. In the royal courts they were the heralds, praise-singers, historians, genealogists, musicians, cheerleaders for those going off to do battle, and they could be dancers, court jesters, and even act as buffoons. As historians they received their greatest reputation.

Griots had their particular modes of dress and unique customs. A *boubou* is a sort of full caftan worn by men and women. A *pagne* is a length of material wound around the body to make a skirt and is worn under a *boubou*. A *chechia* is a scarf worn around the neck. *Gris-gris* is an amulet or good luck charm.

Wandering minstrel and musician *griots* were prohibited from religious burial. Accordingly, *griots* buried their dead in the hollow trunks of the baobab tree because the Wolofs believed that the bodies of *griots* decomposed more rapidly than others, thus contaminating the soil and provoking a famine. Fary's hope that by marrying Prince Bocar she might be able to secure religious burial for *griots* did not overcome her revulsion at his ugly appearance, but it made her determined to marry him in spite of it.

* * *

Fary's father, Mayacine, and the mother of Prince Bocar felt it necessary to consult a *marabout*, a holy man or mystic. (*Marabouts* lived apart and, though not of the ruling class, were influential as counselors.)

Prince Bocar's mother, like all Queen-Mothers, was a very powerful woman. The mother (or, in her absence, a sister or cousin) of a prince or king was known as the *lingeer* and was the most important woman in Wolof society. She usually had a province to tax as her own source of income. Though the first wife of a king or prince had her special title and important privileges, it was the *lingeer* who pulled the strings. In the real world she would not have relinquished one speck of her prerogatives to her daughter-in-law, as Prince Bocar's mother did.

Considering the rigidity of the class system in Wolof society, Fary's marriage to Prince Bocar is more unlikely than Cinderella's to Prince Charming. The union of a *griotte* with a prince was more than unthinkable; it was impossible. And, unlike the transformed Frog Prince in medieval European stories, Prince Bocar does not become any less repulsive after Fary's kiss.

Nevertheless, we all revel in the stories of the naturally noble, though lowly born, who ascend to the loftiest heights through their beauty, pluck, luck, or wit, and so...

Let the *griot* begin:

Bard:	*It used to be told...*
Response:	*It is told...*
Bard:	*There was once...*
Response:	*There will be again...*
Bard:	*It is said that once upon a time...*

Barbara Hetzner Scherer

With special thanks to Dr. Lucie Colvin, University of Maryland, Baltimore County, "Wolof Social Structure as Reflected in the Genesis and Content of the Traditional Literature", Draft presented at the African Studies Association Annual Meeting, October 30, 1974 on the panel "African Intellectual," chaired by Victor A. Olorunsola.

It had been raining incessantly since dawn. The rain went through the roof and fell on Fary. There was thunder and the vociferous storm tore off roofs and mutilated trees. Lightning criss-crossing the sky was suddenly transformed into an immense brazier, a chain of volcanoes whose craters opened like enormous mouths, slobbering with rage, painting the sky with bloody streams of lava. How vain their efforts had been!

For days on end father, mother, brothers, and sisters, their backs bent, had collected, dried, assembled, and tied up the straw to patch the holes in the roofs and avoid serious damage to it.

Huddled in her corner, her *pagne* pulled up to her chin, shivering from the cold and dampness, Fary, undaunted, waited for dawn.

Her parents' bed was separated from hers by a hanging mat which squeaked incessantly in the wind. They were sleeping soundly, the sleep of the just. Her father snored; high and low sounds like the bellows from a forge came from his bed.

Modou, Yandé, Yaram, Biram, and Tior were Fary's brothers and sisters. Crowding in with them was Astou, her cousin on her mother's side who had been entrusted to her mother since childhood. A pestilential odor arose from their humid rags, an odd mixture of dirt, feces, and urine. Pinching her nostrils with two fingers, Fary fought the waves of nausea rising in her. She tore off her old *pagne*, faded, full of holes and mended in many places, and sniffed it all over to detect one of those shameful odors on it. Reassured, her hands still trembling, she lay back down.

Noises came from her parents' bed. Imperceptible at first, they gradually intensified. Heavy breathing, sighs, cries, panting, and murmurs made her keep so still in her bed that her body became numb. She ignored the mosquitoes, ants, and bedbugs who chose this moment to land on her half-naked body. She was afraid to disturb the nocturnal privacy of the adults, to cast doubts into their hearts. At this hour she was supposed to be sleeping soundly in the innocence and peace of childhood.

Little by little, silence returned to the room. Her father's snoring announced the end of the intimacies. Fary relaxed and moved her limbs, which were no longer numb. She was not at all sleepy. Her mind was wide-awake and noted every noise, all of which each night were as one with the darkness.

There were the rats right under her windows, gnawing away on the yams, sweet potatoes, millet stalks, and ears of corn stolen in the field. Each night the mice meticulously deposited their little heaps of droppings. She cursed them. Mocking her traps and poison, they accomplished this ritual, defying her efforts and laughing at her helplessness.

The mice were chasing each other. In their erratic race they touched her nude body with astonishing quickness, smelled her hands, and nibbled at her fingertips which still had a few grains of cous-cous on them. They penetrated baskets, rummaged in boxes, and did somersaults in the trunks. And then, after a most frantic marathon and devilish round, they disappeared into their mysterious hiding places.

The crickets were chirping. Their incessant, strident noise hammered in her temples and resounded in her head like a drum.

The sinister laugh of the hyena made her hair stand on end and her skin bristle with gooseflesh. She shivered when she heard its voice. She prayed as its diabolical laughter announced misfortune.

Then there were the voices. Voices, sometimes high-pitched like the sound of a flute, muted like the steps of the ancestor on the moss, or heavy like the galloping of horses, completed the concert of the night.

At the end of some unreckonable time, noises and voices ceased, going gradually like the reflux of a wave towards the open sea, flowing away as if by a miracle, wrapped in the unfathomable veil of oblivion. But what were they, compared to the perpetual noise, the obsessing cacophony resounding in her head? A grain of sand, a tiny misery drowned in an ocean of shame when compared to the injustice, bitterness, and hate endured by her people for generations.

The cock crowed and the muezzin called the faithful to prayer. Her father's voice, still full of sleep, rose, "Wife, wake up, the cock has crowed."

Fary turned over. A hole in the screen, doubtless the nocturnal work of the rats, caught her eye. A morbid curiosity pushed her to violate the wall separating her from her parents. Her eyes glued to the hole in the screen, she could observe the sacred domain at her leisure. Her father stretched; his joints cracked. His imposing figure filled the bed. His body, nude to the waist, disappeared under the dark *pagne.* His long feet hung over the edge of the bed. After a tremendous yawn, he gave thanks to the Lord. "Thank you, my Lord, for this night of peace. Grant us a day of peace. May it be so for a long time. Amen."

Then he relaxed for a few more minutes. His wife got up and adjusted her *pagne.* But, instead of going out of the house as Fary had expected, she bent over her father and began to massage him. Her skinny breasts hung down. Her stomach was like an empty udder. Her bones stuck out like thorns. Her skinny figure, her lackluster eyes, and the resignation expressed by her whole being symbolized misery.

After accomplishing her morning duty, she woke up her children. She did not coddle them. She slapped their behinds, crying, "Get up! Make the most of the morning breeze. It's a good remedy for poisoned tongues." Fary snored. Her mother stopped next to her for a moment. Her eyes full of indulgence, she stroked Fary's head, murmuring as if she did not dare interrupt her sound sleep, "Fary, Fary, my daughter. Wake up, my little girl."

Fary stretched, yawned, rubbed her eyes, and got up. Her brothers, still asleep, mumbled incoherently. Their mother's voice became firm, then menacing. They quickly got up. Naked as worms, dragging their *pagnes,* they went out into the courtyard, where each of them later tended to his chores.

The village of Mboupbène was spread out over an immense expanse of red, dry, rocky sand. It was dotted here and there with silk-cotton trees, dog mahogany, Spanish Jupiter, palm trees, different varieties of feather grasses, and baobabs which for generations had lifted their branches towards the sky.

Its founder, Sakhor Mboup, was born in Palene-Dede at the court of Damel, the king. His family, descended from the *faras-lambas,* belonged to the famous *griots* of the *Damels* who with their tom-toms and their songs animated the games, the fights, and different court ceremonies. They informed the population about great family events: marriages, deaths, baptisms. Their songs accompanied the rites of passage. They excelled in genealogy and knew everybody's identity. Their tom-toms announced war and peace. They accompanied the kings into battle, praising their courage and that of their ancestors, telling their merits. Enjoying the kings' confidence, *beuk-nek,* faithful servants, they were often asked to intercede with the king to grant special favors.

● ● ●

The ancestor Sakhor Mboup spent his childhood in Palene-Dede where, together with his brother, he learned the tom-tom at an early age. He could not have had a better teacher than his father, who was renowned in the whole country for the cleverness and quality of his play.

At the sudden death of his father, Sakhor Mboup was sent to his uncle who lived in Ndiouki Malik. The uncle was responsible for the initiation of several children, boys and girls, descendants of the *faras-lambas.* Besides being initiated into the chants of the tom-tom, the youngsters received regular courses in history.

Sakhor fell in love with his uncle's daughter, the lovely and charming Yama. Unfortunately, the uncle had greater ambitions for her. His hopes went beyond this young man with empty pockets. In order to discourage the poor young lover, he made his life difficult by making him do endless chores all day long. Faced with these cruel mortifications, the bold young man, encouraged by his love, stole the best horse of his uncle's stable. He stole Yama and fled from Ndiouki. After a long trip, full of danger and rich in emotion, he founded the village of Mboupbène. Today Mboupbène has become a peaceful hamlet with several straw huts uniting various families, who in the course of the years have joined the ancestor in his refuge.

When old Sakhor died, Modou, Fary's grandfather, became chief. At his death, his son Mayacine replaced him. He had four wives. Lala was Fary's mother. Besides these families, there were blacksmiths, shoemakers, jewelers, and weavers living there, all caste brothers of the *griots* who had come to this village seeking the peace and dignity dear to all men.

• • •

A good many of the inhabitants lived around the market. Old Fatim, in her ramshackle hut with its roof almost gone, sat in front of her fruit and roasted peanuts, never stopping to scratch her white head. In the art of misrepresenting her merchandise, she did not have her equal. While the good side of her fruit attracted the eye of the customer, the rotten part was so cleverly hidden that it escaped even the most watchful eye. Her baskets, which appeared very full, were stuffed three-quarters full of old rags. She filled the baskets with the agility of a monkey. Fary often argued with her after she had found out the old woman's misdeeds.

"You ill-brought-up child. Aren't you ashamed, seeing my white hair? I should be surprised to see you live a long time. You like to have too much attention. Your tongue brings misfortune to the wood and even more so to the flesh," she told Fary, menacing her with her fingers.

Zeuma, the Moorish woman, her eternal clay pipe between her lips, offered a variety of beauty aids: *tagout, tousgneul anim,* make-up for eyes and lips, enticing perfumes.

Stranger still was the odor which came from Mame Diarra's dried fish which disappeared under a cloud of enormous green flies whose buzzing was deafening. Contrary to Mame Fatim, Mame Diarra was generosity personified. The victim of rheumatism, she walked little. Fary was often asked to do her errands, particularly to collect firewood. Mame Diarra never got rich for half of her fish ended up in the pots of her errand boys.

Bara, the blacksmith, surrounded by old pots, colanders, pots with holes in them, twisted lances, and broken hoes, was beating his anvil. His watery eyes undressed Fary right to her bone marrow. "Come see me at prayer time. I have something to tell you." She could guess his secret. It was the same with all the young village girls. Usually she refused, but on that day she wanted some money at all costs, for she was going to sneak out to see the witch doctor. So she went into the lion's den, her courage and cunning her only weapons.

She had hardly stepped into the smithy when Bara, surprised, closed the door. He was going to pounce on her when she stopped him cold, yelling, "The money first." Clumsily, he pulled a coin from his pocket, held it out to her with a trembling hand, his face in a contortion that showed his yellow teeth. Fary snatched the money, picked up a cook pot at her feet, and hit the man over the head as hard as she could. He fell down and she ran. Fary was not surprised to hear the next day that Bara had been hurt in a fall when he became faint from the heat in the smithy.

Fara, the shoemaker, made shoes and harnesses for horses. At the moment he was sewing into leather pouches a great number of amulets which the Imam of the mosque distributed to each family in anticipation of the calamities which each year accompanied the rainy season. He adored his work. Nothing would distract him from it. Fara was blind in one eye. Fary and her friends were mad at him for he had refused them the red dye he usually gave them to color their toenails.

On this particular day the little girls played right under Fara's nose. The dust raised by their little feet, which beat the ground furiously, got into the shoemaker's eye and made it teary.

"Go and play somewhere else, you nasty children," he told them, rubbing his good eye. A cloud of dust enveloped him a second time. He got up with his arms outstretched, his feet stumbling in his slippers while the bags and amulets furiously beat against the paint pots which barred his way. In vain Fara tried to find his way in his domain, usually so familiar, but which in a few seconds had become a labyrinth.

Outraged by the rude behavior of the children, of this Fary whose voice he had recognized and who had tricked him for the first time, he was boiling mad. His good eye was full of sand and would not open despite his efforts. Curses followed each other in his throat. *"Domous arame, domous arame,* cursed children," he repeated helplessly.

These legs, these arms, and these bodies, which kept slipping through his hands, maddened him. The little girls attacked him from all sides, clapping their hands and snapping their fingers. Fatou pulled his *boubou* and Astou his *tiaya,* the enormous trousers which billowed like the sail of a ship. In vain Fary and Oumy tried to pull off his bonnet, which Fara kept on by clamping both hands firmly to his head. Fara was spinning around like a top. He gasped and gesticulated like a fish out of water. His misery excited his little torturers whose laughter became louder and louder. Naive and hurtful, they descended upon him like real sledge hammers, showing once again the irresponsibility of childhood. Suddenly there was quiet. Mbarick was passing.

Mbarick was the village idiot. He had been a great fighter and used to be the idol of his generation. He was of colossal stature. According to the old people of Mboupbène, a fight with an evil spirit was the origin of his trouble. His ageless face all but disappeared under a mop of kinky hair full of dust, twigs, food, and parasites. His body, covered with amulets and rags of all sorts, was as black as coal. Some parts of it were covered with deep wounds where children had thrown things at him. His tent was not far from Zeuma, the Moorish woman, and was the stockpile of the market place. *Boubous* and *pagnes* attached to a wooden pole floated in the wind. Calabashes, bowls, and water jugs were piled up. Sometimes there were even chickens and roosters, much to the distress of their rightful owners. Mbarick hated Fary.

On that very day she had managed to retrieve her *pagne*, the only decent one in her wardrobe. She had put it out to dry on the hedge and it had mysteriously found its way into Mbarick's possessions. For five days Fary and circled around the tent, during which time Mbarick had stayed glued to the same spot, defying all tentative approaches of the young girl.

Sitting in the middle of his treasure, a lot of rocks to throw within his reach, his lips were pulled up in an evil smile. His eyes sparkled. They said, "Come on, if you dare." And his hands weighed the stones. Finally, good luck. The whinnying of a horse momentarily distracted the sick man's attention; he turned around. Fary snatched her *pagne* and ran as fast as she could. After a hectic pursuit, Mbarick threw a rock which hit Fary in the face. A scar above her right eye would record the work of the sick man.

In the tent of Baye Daour assembled old and young who were eager for news. This was where intrigues started, where marriages and coalitions were arranged. Here also came the news from the outside world which the newsmonger, who had just arrived, liked to relate in the smallest detail. Afflicted with deafness, Baye Daour had trouble keeping up a conversation. Fary always managed to leave the buying of millet to her brothers and sisters, for every time she was charged with doing it, she came home from the market with her voice gone from too much yelling.

On that morning she said to him, "My mother would like five kilos of millet."

"Oh yes, my daughter's baptism is going to be on Thursday," he answered with a smile that uncovered this three beetle nut-stained teeth.

"I leave the errand to you, Tior. I don't want to be voiceless today. You talk to him about the baobab tree, he shows you the Spanish Jupiter. You see how you get on with him. I'm leaving." Without waiting for her brother's answering and protestations, Fary went away.

Karamokho, the seer and sorcerer, rubbed his shells with left-over crushed cola nuts, and slowly, solemnly wrapped his horns in scarlet cloth. His divine powers made him feared and respected. According to the villagers' stories, he could change human beings into monkeys or dispatch them to the next world with impressive speed. Lala often warned her daughter about him. He was entitled to deference and humility from Fary. Sitting or crouching before him, the people who had come to consult him uneasily awaited his predictions. Fary sat down among them. From the village grapevine she knew their secrets. People gave her evil looks. How pretentious of this child to dare violate a domain reserved for grown-ups. She observed them, indifferent to their disapproval. Not wanting to be recognized, they tried to hide in shawls, bonnets, and *boubous* which did not manage to conceal their identity.

Diama, a young tortured woman whose eyes were in constant motion, looked at the advice-seekers one by one. Barren, she was looking for elusive fertility. Sady, the impotent, mocked by all the women, divorced five times, was looking for a miracle to restore his manhood. Anta, the jealous one, was resolved to do in her pretty rival, Aicha, and to keep her impartial husband to herself. The *cadi*, Tiendou, the usurer, who appropriated the land of the deceased for himself, was trying to silence the lawful heirs.

Karamokho's grave voice caught Fary's attention. He gestured, spoke in a language known only to him, threw the cowries, opened his eyes wide, picked up the cowries, threw them again, squinted, shook his head, and moving his lips, emitted some rumbles from his bowels. He then fell into a deep silence which seemed to last an eternity to all the advice-seekers, who were shaken by this most frightening wait where fear and doubt and apprehension paralyzed them while they waited for his revelations. It was not yet their turn, yet they had trembled as if it had been.

After several minutes of silence he spoke to Aly the baker, whose assistant had stolen his wife. A martyr, he was as skinny as a reed. He was so tense that while he was listening for Karamokho's words, his back resembled a bow ready to be shot from. The prediction was a whopper. Perspiration ran down Aly's shiny, tormented face. His lips trembled. His head fell. Sometimes his hand reached out as if in prayer. Fary kept looking at him. Crying with commiseration, she was on Aly's side with all her heart.

Right after the morning prayers, Fary, with her brothers and sisters, ate the millet mush prepared by one of the wives whose turn it was that day. Fary loathed the mush prepared by Anta, her father's third wife. Anta fed them millet flour that was full of sand and small stones. Her laziness and incompetence endangered the family's health. Fary did not like her at all. Her father was aware of her dislike. His secret penchant for the lazy woman was the reason for the severe looks and harsh words he had for Fary at the slightest provocation.

Fary was in charge of taking the animals out, milking them, and cleaning the common rooms. Yaram and Yandé helped her with the laundry and the dishes. Contrary to tradition, she was also responsible for keeping the sheep, a task most often assigned to boys. Thanks to her efforts, her father could pride himself on owning a choice herd. She had been after him to buy the much-coveted ram of the deceased Laba, which his heirs were in a hurry to sell the day after the funeral. Fary jealously took care of the sheep, always trying to do better than her father, who shared her passion for them. Secretly she had named them all, but she called them by name only when they were away in a far pasture, where alone with them, she would talk to them, scold, laugh out loud, or sometimes even, with her shepherd's staff, give them a regular thrashing when they had transgressed her rules.

They were milked daily, the first claim to the milk belonging to her father. The fresh eggs collected in the chicken coop were for him, but he was not counting on the dunning of the children! A good part disappeared, smuggled out with the trash of the common rooms.

The chore of fetching the water fell to the boys. They went to get it at the well of Mbayane, two miles from Mboupbène. They often complained about the distance, but did not dare protest in front of their father; however, as soon as his back was turned, they argued vehemently about the paternal rule which freed the girls from this chore.

"Where is the preferential treatment you are talking about?" Fary asked roughly one day when she surprised them in their bitter complaints.

"You get the water, we get the washing, the cooking, the household chores. It's the girls who have something to complain about. What are eight kilometers back and forth compared to the chores we do all day long?"

Taken aback by her words and the loudness of her voice, they fearfully looked left and right, afraid that their father might suddenly appear. Full of hate, they gave their sister long, angry looks before they disappeared into the forest.

• • •

After their various chores at home, they went out into the fields. Fary carried the mush securely fastened on her head. Her cousin Astou and her sisters carried gourds of water. Her brothers had long knives, machetes, hoes, and rakes. They were barely clothed. Their bare feet, calloused and impervious to the thorns or the boiling heat of the sand, went over the ground as fast as snakes. Their father, on horseback, a *pagne* on his head to protect him from the sun, followed them peaceably.

The field was divided into several parts; here millet was grown. An enormous scarecrow reigned in the midst of the stalks and kept away the birds who had already begun to eat the young shoots. The scarecrow, fashioned by Fary, had more than once fooled the eyes of passers-by, who, taking it for Mayacine, gave it their more respectful salutes and most reverent curtsies. Mayacine, furious with such lack of respect, had more than once meant to scold his daughter, but, at the last moment, overcome by Fary's cleverness, for her work of art was perfect, had thought better of it. The resemblance was striking, so striking that he found it difficult to keep his equanimity when faced with his image. The head had been covered with his old bonnet which had disappeared a long time ago. His *tiaya,* his full trousers, had been given away to Mor the beggar, and now accentuated the roundness of the figure's behind. His short shirt, which he had lost sight of over a year ago and quarreled over violently with Lala, did not quite reach the waistline and showed a bulging stomach.

Here there were *niebe,* broad beans. Rampant, spread out in a carpet of green leaves, touched with spots of purple, they gleamed in the sun. A little further, yams. Little bushes swayed in the wind; their narrow stalks bowed left and right in graceful curtsies, kissing the newly tilled ground. Over there, peanuts; they spread out to infinity in countless little green bouquets decorated with golden buds. Palmyras, standing here and there in the field, majestically lifted their interminable trunks towards heaven, crowned by clusters of fruit, the lacy leaves standing out in the immense blue dome of the sky.

A cabin built in the shadiest spot received them for their noon break. Their father spent most of his time there, stretched out in his hammock, gently rocked by the breezes, escaping the dense foliage of the mango trees. His snoring could be heard by the children with their backs bent and their feet on fire as they covered the holes filled with seeds.

• • •

Fary, in spite of herself, had to accept this difference in social hierarchy which made her father a king, his wives and children slaves. He always had the best part, the good meals, the best clothes, the best bed. He had a right to rest, to be massaged. He could get angry, insult them, beat them; he still was always shown respect and consideration.

"This superiority of the man," her mother told her, which was undoubtedly questioned elsewhere, "is never disputed in Mboupbène. It goes back many years to when our ancestor Yam Mademba Khary Mboup was repudiated and banished from the clan.

"On that day Yam's husband, Samba Mar Dialo Mboup, showed the door to the rich Laba, a suitor for their daughter's hand. He was the most sought-after catch of the region. Yam, afraid of losing this good match, dared to speak up in front of her lord and master."

" 'Uncle, why this refusal, what do you have against Laba? Is he not rich? Is he not of our blood? This is a big chance for our daughter. Don't you see the hand of fate which has led him to our humble home?'

"The man, astonished by his wife's audacity, was furious. Beside himself with rage, he advanced towards her menacingly, when in his anger he turned over the big pot where the family supper was cooking. He fell headlong to the floor, scalded by the boiling water from which white clouds of steam rose to the sky. He screamed with all his might. The family was there, paralyzed, incapable of moving or coming to his help, hypnotized by the pain the head of the family was suffering, but also shamed by the indecency of the situation. His torn pants offered the most irreverent sight the family ever had to face.

"His oldest son finally reacted. He caught his father by the shoulders and pulled him out of the slippery puddle which slowly spread to the courtyard. He was limp now. A week later he died of the burns he had sustained. The cursed wife was chased out of the house by the dead man's family. A chant accompanied her departure. One often hears it during ceremonies or during contests opposing the community of Mboupbène to the descendants of the ancestor. From then on, submission to the man has become our rule."

Lala was small and unobtrusive. She accomplished her daily chores with submissiveness, serenity, and perseverance. Her skeletal body was surely the result of physical exhaustion, but more probably was due to her moral suffering which gnawed at her like a malignancy, whose name was Astou. Astou was her niece. She had been entrusted to her when her mother died in childbirth. Fary did not like Astou at all. More than once had she surprised her in conversation with Anta, discrediting Lala. Poor Anta! She did not in the least suspect what this snake in the grass had in store for her. The perverse girl had eyes on Anta's husband. Her respectful manners and her humble and innocent ways did not fool Fary. When Astou was alone with her father, she brushed against him with her firm young breasts, wiggled her behind, and looked at him longingly. Mayacine ignored her or pretended to ignore her, but the impertinent girl kept it up.

On that particular day Astou had kept to her bed. Mayacine, who had to go to old Bacar's funeral, did not go to the fields. Lala in her haste had forgotten part of the seeds. Halfway to the fields she remembered. Fary turned around and went home. Surprise! Her father was in her mother's bed holding Astou's breast as she gazed at him. Mayacine looked up and saw his daughter. Not at all embarrassed, Astou gave her a smile. Fary's heart jumped in her breast. She was torn by disgust and a terrible jealousy. The disdain and the determination in her face kept her father from slapping her. She took the seeds and left. She cried for a long time, but kept her secret.

● ● ●

A few days after this incident, the fourth wife was renounced. Her mush was too salty. Astou took her place. She made life miserable for Lala, whose shame was slowly killing her. In connivance with her brothers and sisters, Fary revenged her mother in her own way. Astou's poultry was mistreated, her *pagnes* cut up, her meals oversalted. Her father did his utmost to replace the wardrobe after each incident and to ignore the bad meals, but he had not counted on the children's determination. He never managed to catch them in the act.

On that particular day their father's deep voice pulled the children suddenly out of their sleep. Sensing some misfortune, for this was the first time in her life that her mother's soft voice had not awakened her, Fary ran towards the screen and lifted it. Her mother cowered in bed, trembling like a leaf, her body covered with perspiration. A cough rose from her throat like a complaint. Her father left the room to go over to Astou. Fary woke up her grandmother to tell her about her daughter's sudden illness.

Then Fary went into the forest to gather herbs which she put on her mother's body to make the fever go down. Her brothers and sisters were crying, "she is going to die, she is going to die," their eyes haggard. Fary reassured them the best she could, and with great courage took over the family. She gave orders and shared the work with an energy born of despair. Surprised by her authority, her brothers and sisters obediently did the tasks she assigned to them. After a few days of acute illness, Lala began to convalesce.

One morning when Fary straightened her bedcloths, her mother took her hand and whispered, "Daughter, come to see me when you have finished your work. Try to see to it that we are not disturbed. I want to talk to you."

Her father had suddenly become invisible, and appeared at the doorstep for a few seconds to inquire about the sick woman only if he happened to remember. Astou was expecting a child. Her nausea, her vomiting and her dizzy spells manifested themselves with violence even though her belly was still as flat as a board. Mayacine surrounded her with charms and all sorts of attentions to see to the end of this pregnancy which ill-intentioned rivals wanted to destroy at all costs. Fary was ashamed. Her father, even though he had enough children to form a regiment, acted as if he were expecting his first child.

● ● ●

"Here I am, mother. We are alone. The family is in the fields. The 'snake' has gone out, probably to buy another talisman."

"Fary, if you want to please me, leave her alone. The blood of the chicken only soils the fingers of the one who kills it. I was wrong to have nourished an adder at my bosom. Who will live shall see. God is just. Forget Astou for now and listen to me carefully. Do you know the principality of Tiali?"

Fary opened her eyes wide. She had not expected such a question.

"No, mother. I have only heard speak of it. It seems it is a wonderful place. But I don't like the prince who, just as he likes, can take away our best rams."

"That is his right, my daughter. We are his subjects and we in Mboupbène more so than others for we are also his *griots*. Tiali is governed by prince Bocar Djiwan Malik who is one of Ndiamal Djiwan's grandsons. Ndiamal had twelve sons. He set them up in twelve regions to which he gave their names and first names. His son Bocar received the county of Tiali. This is how Tiali Malick Bocar was founded. It is a day and a half's ride on horseback from Mboupbène. We depend on Bocar. If he has the goodness not to claim big yearly contributions, he can take a few animals from time to time for the needs of the court.

"When Bour Sine married his daughter, the prince was invited to the ceremony. He came back with one of the most humiliating and abject innovations for us as Muslims and as human beings. These terrible pagans bury their *griots* in tree trunks to ward off catastrophes. Putting them in one ground, they say, invites disasters such as lightning, drought, and earthquakes.

"Bocar Djiwan Malick has assigned the cursed baobabs east of Mboupbène to the members of our caste. From now on, these trees will be our cemetery. The prince has posted his policemen here to ensure that this new law is applied. Some people who thought they were more clever than others tried to bury their dead quickly in the fields or behind their fences during the night. They were found out and severely punished.

"You must wonder why I tell you all this. It is because I am afraid. Yes, I am afraid. I dreamed I saw myself thrown into this tree trunk. I can't sleep anymore when I think that my body will never know our traditional resting place, but in its place this pagan rite which is against our religion. It weighed like a stone on my head. Now I feel relieved since I have spoken to you."

● ● ●

Fary was speechless. The stone had moved from her mother's heart onto the daughter's. She left her mother and went to find Coura, her cousin on her father's side, her friend and only confidante. She told her about the talk she had had with her mother. Coura could scarcely believe it. Neither of them knew about the cemetery.

Children, especially girls, never followed a funeral procession. Full of curiosity, they decided to hide in an adjoining field to see a funeral which was to take place that day.

They were barely hidden behind the trees when they heard the incantations with the words *"Allah! Allah!"* repeated incessantly. Some men carried the body of the deceased on their shoulders. They put it at the foot of the baobab and stood facing it. They prayed standing up without prostrating themselves, and repeated in chorus, *"Allakhou akbar!"* as if they were celebrating some strange rite. After a resounding *"Assala Malekoum,"* they took the body, wrapped it in a white shroud, and murmured while they put it in the hole, "You can see us, our Lord. We respect you and adore you. We believe in your messenger, the Prophet Mohammed. May peace be with him. This act is an order from down here below. It does not change our faith. May your clemency and your pity accompany him."

Coura shivered; she was crying. Tears streamed down her smooth cheeks and fell in the cleavage of her young breasts shaped like papayas. From time to time her shoulders raised in a sob. She fought to suppress her emotion which made her eyes squint and pulled her lips into an ugly grimace. Fary moved close to her trying to comfort her, but she could hardly manage it. She was so moved that she was speechless. Her eyes were full of love and compassion when she looked at Coura. Better than her voice and lips could have done, her eyes expressed a consoling sympathy. She finally broke the silence.

"Coura, I should like to ask you a question which no one has been able to answer for me. I have heard explanations here and there. I have overheard conversations that were more or less evasive; I have listened at doors. I have discussed it with my mother and the elders, but I still don't know. You, whose father is a very wise man, can you tell me why we are different from other people? How have we come by this inheritance? How did we become *griots* and people of caste?"

"Fary, to be honest, I can only repeat my father's words. He often speaks of the right of man, of the equality of human beings as described in the Koran. This equality exists in the holy places of people from the world over, no matter what country they come from, what their color or race, regardless of their birth or attributes, they all wear the same white garment as a symbol of equality, of anonymity on this earth."

"Coura, this white garb, this muslim rite is not known to the pagans that rule us."

"Fary, stop being difficult just for once. You asked me for an explanation and I am telling you exactly what my father said. You can believe it or not, just as you like. Either you are going to listen to me or I keep silent. What we have just seen has upset me. I am in no mood to argue."

"Go ahead. I'm listening."

"A long time ago, a very long time ago, my father says, people lived in wide open spaces, settled around a chief in order better to protect themselves against dangers. They domesticated animals, grew plants, and divided the work. For the sake of harmony in their lives, they divided into several groups. Some specialized in fishing or hunting. Others became weavers. This division of labor later turned into a social hierarchy, which, with the *ouoloffs*, was the origin of these classifications."

"The nobles were the *guerrs*, the jewelers the *teugnes*, the woodworkers were called *laobes*, the shoemakers became the *oudes*, the weavers the *rabes* and the slaves took the name of *diam*. We the *griots* are what we are, *Ngueol*.

"Except for the privileged class of the *guerr*, we travel in the same ship as our brothers. We are once again people of caste. To aspire to an alliance, be it male or female, with one of these beings of so-called superior origin, would be folly."

Once again Fary was speechless. Emotions of pain and helplessness choked her. She felt as if she would burst. Her heart expanded and contracted in her chest like a spring. This injustice had pitilessly destroyed her. With a great concentration of will, she ceased her laments. Terror was reflected on her face, followed by an expression of indescribable hatred. She was deadly angry at her ancestors who had fatalistically accepted the condition of slavery instead of refusing this inferior condition imposed on them by a domineering society. It was a real affront to human dignity. She, Fary, was a woman of caste, a *griotte*. Her world was forever limited to the tiny circle of her race.

She became ill. The fever brought her down. One nightmare followed another in her burning head. Tree branches picked her up like the arms of an octopus and threw her into an immense black hole. She cried; she was choking. She fought against the invisible powers; she turned over and over, caught in a trembling that became a delirium.

Fary's illness became her mother's best remedy. She forgot

her own sorrow to watch over Fary. The *marabouts* outdid each other finding remedies for her. She had seen what she must not see. She was possessed. One had to wash her face and close her eyes so that henceforth she could not see beyond the border of the mortals. Some thought it was the *djins,* the spirit, the *couyoum djin,* the male, the master of the *djins,* which lived in her small body. They had to be exorcised through incantations, concoctions, and incense. After two full weeks she was once again able to do her chores.

Sokhna was Coura's aunt. Her house, incontestably the most beautiful in Mboupbêne, had brought her the nickname, "moneybags." Divorced a long time, she led a gay life. She was thought to have had a few adventures and her reputation was not spotless. Unbeknownst to her parents, Fary often went to see Sokhna because she had cowrie shells which never lied and also because of the few pennies Sokhna would give Fary on these occasions.

Her big house, hung with *pagnes,* always smelled of incense. Pretty mats covered the floor. A big bed covered with a colorful spread filled half the room. Sokhna was tall and strong. Her walk was graceful and her voice as soft and modulated as a lullaby. She had a whole string of admirers, of whom Mayoro was first in the running.

Fary and Coura came to consult her because their future worried them. Up to now there had not been one suitor on the horizon, even though marriage age rapidly approached. They had been careful not to reveal the real reasons for the consultation, leaving it to the ingenious Sokhna to ask her cowries.

A little maliciously she asked the girls, "What brings you here?"

"We want to consult your cowries for the usual sacrifices at the harvest dance."

Sokhna's eyes sparkled. She was not fooled. "Sacrifice, yes. But for what? For the harvest or for the men?

"Whose turn first?"

"Fary's," answered Coura.

Fary stepped forward, trembling, her heart beating fast as it always did when she was going to learn about her destiny. She made her wishes, blew on the cowries, and threw them into the tray.

"You will give soured milk to the children on Thursday. Two cola nuts, one white, one red, to an old woman."

Fary hoped that the alms she must give would stop right there for her meager purse could not provide any more. And no more chances to get money from Bara!

"A young man of fair complexion, handsome, a scar on the right ear, here, right in front of you," Sokhna said, pushing a cowrie towards Fary. Her forehead wrinkled, her face serious, she continued, "A little man, fat. black. ugly but rich, even extremely rich, a prince, at any rate. A big name, right in front of you. Enormous wealth here, all around you.

"Ah," she said after a short silence, "This little cowrie is between you and all those riches and that man in front of you. But all this eliminated," she said, sweeping up the cowrie of bad omen, "fortune will smile on you." She looked at Fary as if seeing her for the first time, threw her cowries and looked at her again.

"Yes, Fary, three times thrown. Three times the cowries showed the same thing. You will be a princess. I swear by my ancestors that people will prostrate themselves before you. That is, if you manage to clear away this obstacle on your way," she said, angrily pushing away the small cowrie.

"Could you tell me the nature of this obstacle?" Fary asked in a trembling voice.

"There might be several things. Offerings to be made, animals to be immolated, alms to be given. Let me look once more."

She threw the cowries and said, "It is neither a sacrifice nor alms to be given. It is a human being, more precisely a woman who stands in your way. She is the concrete to be poured, the tree to be felled, the obstacle to overcome to get at this fortune and this man."

"Will I get at it?" Fary asked, overexcited.

Again Sokhna gathered her cowries, consulted them, murmuring incantations.

"Probably yes, certainly yes, but not without great difficulties."

For a moment Fary abandoned herself to the predictions. Her eyes closed, she saw herself a princess. It lasted only a few seconds, then she was frightened.

"Coura, does this happy prediction not hide some misfortune? Did she not see my death? Old Fatim always predicts my early demise. And this woman in my path, wouldn't she be a *djin?*"

"No, Fary, she saw you as a princess, so don't worry. I don't know how it's going to happen, but happen it will. Her conclusion is the only thing that counts. That's what's essential. I believe in her. Her knowledge of the cowries is inherited. Her ancestor, who was known to all the princes, bequeathed her his knowledge. He chose her over the males in the family for the spirits saw in her the real repository of the spiritual powers. Make your sacrifices. We will see what happens."

"I can't believe it, Coura."

"Why shouldn't you be a princess, Fary? Kings have married *griottes* before. Why not you? Don't underestimate your beauty. It is exceptional."

"I must keep my feet on the ground. This sort of thing does not happen to a girl of my race. With the little bait I have, how could I land such a fish? Can you see me as a princess, me, Fary Mboup, *griotte,* untouchable, a woman of caste for generations, whose only wealth is this so-called beauty and a moth-eaten *pagne* around her hips! She is really good, but I'm afraid that today the spirits are not with her or are hiding something from her."

"If I didn't know you better, Fary," I would think you were cynical. I assure you that you will be a princess. Who wouldn't like that, my friend? It's the dream of every young girl, the realization of all dreams, wealth, jewels, clothes and honor."

"To become rich, me who never knew anything but poverty. What luck!" The words danced in her head. "Imagine, Coura, hundreds of slaves kissing the feet of Fary Mayacine Mboup? No, it's just a dream, but what munificence for my family and all the relatives!" Then she fell silent.

"What's the matter?" Coura asked, her eyes still bright with joy and excitement.

"Remember Sokhna's words? 'A small man, fat, black, ugly?' I hate ugliness."

"Don't jump to conclusions. Let's wait and when the time comes, we shall see. Besides, what does physical beauty matter in a man? In my opinion, it's the heart which is more important."

Mayacine often went to Tiali to give an account to the prince of all that went on in Mboupbène. These absences did not at all please Astou, who at the moment was more of a princess than Fary.

"Mayacine," she told her husband when he came home, "this is the fourth time you have skipped my turn. Why should your other wives enjoy your company twice a week? What have they got that I haven't got? The prince of Tiali always chooses *my* turn to call you to his side. You would think he does it on purpose. You are hardly better than his slaves. Do you have to hold the candle when he fulfills his obligations to his wives? Does he need your help so much? Answer me. You also have obligations to your wives, especially to me who is only sixteen years old. If you can't fulfill these obligations, I am going back to my parents."

Worn out by his long trip, surprised by this most insulting and amazingly humiliating reception, Mayacine raised the whip he still held and was going to hit Astou. Seeing his children there, their eyes lowered, he stopped short. His voice permitted no reply.

"Woman, in all my life I have not met anyone so rude, so perverse, and so abject and ill brought-up as you. You dare to blaspheme and berate my prince. You dare to insult me, your husband, your master. Pack your bags. From this moment on you mean nothing to me. Leave this house before I can no longer answer for myself, before I am obliged to kill you."

Astou, taken aback by her husband's words, nevertheless stood her ground, pointing to her swollen belly, and cried and carried on with all her might. Her frightened eyes went from child to child. Mayacine lifted his hand and a mighty slap resounded on the young woman's cheek. She started to laugh, looked at the children again, started to whine, and then to sob. Then, her hands on her waist, she twisted in pain. The generous Lala, forgetting the fate of her ancestor Yam Mademba Khary Mboup, interceded with her husband.

"Uncle, I beg you on my knees to keep her until she has the baby. Her grandparents live far away. She will be delivered prematurely."

"So be it." Mayacine answered. "She is acting. She is bluffing as usual. She won't spend the night here. Whoever gives her the slightest help will leave the house with her."

He threw her clothes and pots and pans into the courtyard. Her head bent, Astou went away. Fary was proud of her father who, as the master, had finally made a decision long overdue.

On the occasion of the new moon a week of festivities, matches, dances, and chants had been organized in Mboupbène. On that occasion Fary met the man around on whom all her thoughts would now center. She noticed him in a group of spectators who were intently watching the fighters. She could not stop looking at his handsome face. There was a scar on the right ear. Sokhna's prediction was coming true. Their eyes sought each other and held each other in the light of the huge bonfire. Fary's heart was beating so fast it frightened her. She went away, ashamed of her strong emotions, and went to look for Coura.

"Are you ill? Have you seen a ghost?"

"No, nothing like that," she answered in a choking voice. "Follow me!" She pulled her friend behind a tree from where she could observe the object of her emotion.

"Ah, I see. Don't worry, you are not the only one. He breaks hearts wherever he goes. The young girls are smitten and the women sin. It's hard to resist his look. It's Gana Mboup, the son of Baye Daour the deaf man. Didn't you hear about the big fight the girls had over him last Thursday down by the river? It was a bloody battle where they tore each other's *pagnes*, hair and ears and threw rocks and shouted insanities. And yet, at night he is not so handsome. You must look at him tomorrow, in daylight. Try not to faint."

"What a surprise, Coura! Baye Daour's son? Such a beauty. How did that old deaf man produce such a marvel?"

"Be a little more charitable. Daour is old, but you can still see the traces of how handsome he was, even though he has lost all of his teeth. We'll see what happens to the son when he is his father's age. May God grant us a long life."

Fary was beautiful. She had that beauty which is authentically black, wild, pure, and enchanting. A black complexion, not a muddy black but a healthy clarity, shiny, and flawless, brightened by teeth that a kind nature had lined up in absolute perfection. Her eyes were lively, clear, a bit cunning and charming, her nose pert. Her eyes were full of fun and belied her submissive bearing. Her lips were sensual and would have moved a heart of stone. Gana, like many others, was receptive to so much charm. Fary was in love and was loved in return and lived only for the moments when they could meet in secret. For the moment, Gana was her prince.

For the celebration of the annual feast of Tiali, Mayacine had been ordered by the prince, Bocar, to bring, as in years past, a herd of one hundred rams chosen among the finest of Mboupbène. Three Peul herdsmen, Biram, Tior, and Fary were to accompany Mayacine on that expedition. Fary was in charge of the food. For the first time in the history of Mboupbène, a member of the so-called weaker sex was granted this honor. The determination, the maturity, initiative, and courage Fary had shown during her mother's illness, the good care she took of the rams plus the many questions she had asked her father about Tiali were undoubtedly the reason for her being allowed to go. She was surprised, excited, and happy.

● ● ●

They left Mboupbène at daybreak as soon as the animals had been gathered. After the blessing by the Imam, Mayacine, armed with a shotgun, rode at the head of the convoy. Fary rode next to him, the food and kitchen utensils in her saddle bags. Her body was bent under the many charms her mother, in tears, had put on her to protect her from the dangers of the journey.

Biram and Tior, bow and arrows slung over their shoulders, clumsily held the guns their father had given them. They were going to be using them for the first time in their lives. The two Peuls helped the brothers on either side of the herd. They were dressed in short blue *boubous;* two long braids starting at the top of their heads hung down to their shoulders. They had bows, but disdained guns, preferring clubs, machetes, and cutlasses. The third Peul closed the march. The journey was supposed to last five days.

The first day passed without any incident. They were bothered only by unusual heat which a leaden sun poured over them. They went through dense bush which did not resist the machetes of the herdsmen. Towards noon they stopped near a waterhole. The herd grazed on the carpet of green grass spread under their feet and drank from the waterhole. Biram and Tior collected dry wood. Fary made a mush of millet, roasted peanuts, and beans. They rested until the second prayer of the day in the midst of a frantic concert coming out of the dense tree branches.

They went on. Frightened rabbits ran into the bush; squirrels, impossible to catch, appeared, disappeared, reappeared quick as lightning. Guinea hens were chasing each other. Red monkeys adroitly took away the band's peanuts. Whole swarms of birds, bullfinches, red-breasted robins, and white-winged warblers flew over them, unfolding their multicolored wings over their heads like umbrellas. Sometimes they landed on the rams and teased them with their beaks. From time to time they saw peacocks strutting, their tails spread out in a burst of color, majestic as plumed helmets.

After the prayer of the day, Mayacine sent Ardo, the chief herdsman, to inspect the area in order to find a suitable place to spend the night. He came back after one hour. They were in an immense stretch of red sand with little vegetation where a ball of fire descended on the horizon. They collected dry firewood.

After a frugal meal of two grilled guinea hens, their father's bounty, they enclosed the herd in a big circle made of branches and lit a big fire in the middle.

A watch was organized for the night. Fary was excluded from it. Her father took the first shift. Stretched out not far from him, she kept watching him. His loaded shotgun by his side, he kept lighting his pipe. He was nervous. His head turned, his ears perked; he was waiting for those alarm signals of innumerable, strangely menacing, discordant noises of the jungle. Tension emanated from him like a fluid, was in the air, reached Fary, and became one with her. She too was filled with anguish, this tickling in her hands, the stinging sensation in her eyes, this perspiration which makes the whole body clammy, the water running down the armpits, the forehead, the neck, this spasm that violently grips the spine, the intense thirst that dries up your throat, the bitter taste of bile in your mouth, and the pain in your belly that rises from the intestines to the heart and to the throat, and like a thorn hurts, tears, lacerates, makes you want to vomit, to yell and to disappear before the superiority of the invisible enemy. Barely able to swallow, she rolled over towards her father, finding solace in his strength.

• • •

Mayacine was carefully stoking their fire. Then came the laughter of the hyenas from the south. He jumped; his body relaxed like a spring. He grabbed his shotgun, going into shooting position. Fary kept as still as a corpse. She was the first girl ever to join the convoy and she must be worthy of it. All the incantations she had known from childhood spun in her head, and passed her lips like a stream. The hyenas came closer. She dug her fingernails into her flesh. Her father went straight ahead and away from her. She gnashed her teeth, bit her tongue. Her neck, held in the same position, hurt her terribly. She must in no way attract attention. Her father went on, went on ever farther. Three shots. The sinister cries of the hyenas stopped. Mayacine came back to his place, lit his pipe, and Fary fell soundly asleep.

• • •

At the first sign of dawn they went on their way. Ardo, who had been sent ahead as a scout, came back in a terrifying state. His *boubou* was in shreds, his hair was undone and hanging about his shoulders. The red dust mixed with sweat had turned his beautiful face into a scary mask. The blood ran from his arm where a deep gash had torn his flesh. His machete was red with blood. With unequaled stoicism he stood there, not admitting to any physical weakness despite his obvious state of distress. "I fell into a lion's den. The cubs were alone, but their mother surprised me and attacked. I was hurt; it was either she or I. She escaped. She must have smelled the animals. We might expect a visit."

Mayacine was uneasy. As Ardo was speaking, he started to breathe heavily. This time Fary was in the middle of the enclosure. Her father, anxious for her safety, had assigned her this choice spot. It was a safe location in his opinion, but not in hers. If the animals were attacked, they would all converge on her and squash her like dough. Carefully she looked over the enclosure. Her searching eyes finally detected a little opening through which she could flee in case of danger.

Tior and Samba, the second shepherd, were on watch. Her brother kept polishing his gun which he treated like a relic. Fary became aware of an unusual tension in the herd. The sheep got up, bleated, butted one another about. The horses were pawing the ground. All of these were signs of danger. Ali, the third shepherd, armed with his club, had difficulty in calming them. Ardo took a powder out of his belt, recited an incantation, and sprinkled the powder around. A rabbit crossed in front of them. Tior fired his first shot which made his father's *chechia* fly. The lioness came upon them like lightning. She jumped on Tior, her fangs bared, foaming at the mouth, claws outstretched. Samba stopped her with a stroke of the matchete. The terrified herd tried to escape in every direction. Tior shook all over.

In a paroxysm Fary thought she was going to die, disemboweled by the horns of the rams all coming together over her. No more emergency exit.

She yelled with all her might, when she felt strong arms lifting her up just as she lost consciousness. Bent over her, her father sprayed her with water and made her smell a rag soaked with animals' urine. Tior was still shaking. He shook so much that he carried his father, who was holding him, in a strange clasp with him. They moved in a diabolical dance, one step here, two steps there. Ardo tore Tior out of his father's arms and slapped him brutally in the face. Tior opened his eyes wide and began to laugh, a demented laughter which frightened Fary. Her brother was going mad. Mayacine felt compassion and went towards him when Ardo stopped him with a look.

"Leave him alone. He is a man. He will get over it."

They broke camp and went on their way.

• • •

On the third day of their journey they met some nomadic

shepherds who were trekking with their herds. There were interminable greetings between Ardo and his companions, incompre-
hensible palavers in front of calabashes of hot milk offered
generously in the round huts. These were guesthouses built here
and there in the jungle to house the herdsmen on the move with
their cattle.

Still, on the third day, after they had left the herdsmen, they
heard a terrible racket, chants, laughter, a veritable bedlam:
hunters. They were naked. A loincloth with colorful fringes between
their legs was their only clothing. Lion and panther heads, the
totem of their clan, were painted on their powerful chests and their
broad, muscled backs. Hung with charms, carrying bows and
arrows, virile and terrifying under their clay masks, two-by-two they
carried between two poles the deer they had hunted. Their bags
were overflowing with guinea hens, wild ducks, and hares.

Fary kept her distance. Their get-up, the wildness, and the
strength they exuded, made them exceptional beings. Yet they
approached their group with exuberance. Fraternally they shared
generously the fruit of their labors and courage. Then the echo of
the chants disappeared in the depths of the jungle.

On that same day, so rich in adventure, they had to cross a
lake, the home of the great Boa, the guardian spirit of the region.
To violate this water was sacrilege. In the claws of fear they felt like
offerings on the altar. Each one felt as if he were about to be
immolated.

Ardo took a calabash which he filled with the milk he carried
with him in an udder. He lifted his hands towards heaven, recited
incantations, poured some of the milk into the lake, and threw in
three white cola nuts and seven cowrie shells. They all rubbed their
bodies with the rest of the milk the shepherd had mixed with a
special powder.

Ardo took the lead of the convoy with the herd. The others
followed in single file, shotguns and food on their heads. The water
came up to their waists. Finally, they reached the opposite bank
without mishap. Fary from then on paid closer attention to the Peul
herdsmen.

The Peuls lived in a world of their own. They played strange
melodies on their flutes while their islamic companions prostrated
themselves towards the East to glorify the Lord. Taciturn, they
mostly conversed among themselves in a singsong nasal dialect.
They ate little, and drank milk which came out of the udders they

carried as if by magic. They hardly ever slept; their endurance was beyond belief. They ignored Islam. Their incantations and prayers were addressed to the spirits rather than to a single god.

They had a very light complexion, almost white, were tall and wiry, and as supple as lynxes. Their finely chiseled faces were hardened by a penetrating look and black lips whose tattoos attested to their courage and daring.

• • •

On the fourth day they crossed a wooded area, dense and almost unreal in this plain. Innumerable monkeys appeared in families, the male at the head of the line, followed by females with their young on their bellies. Others, hanging in the treetops, pelted them with seeds. They could not ride their horses on the narrow paths; the Peuls led the animals by their bridles.

A snake bit Biram. While Mayacine and his children awkwardly tried to get through the brush to come to his help, Ardo was already at Biram's feet. His mouth, applied to the wound, drew out some black blood which he spat out at once. Biram, stretched out on the ground, was covered with sweat. He sobbed and twisted his body in all directions. Bloody foam came from his lips. Ardo enlarged the wound with his cutlass and poured in a powder which he carried in his belt along with a great variety of other medication. Once again incantations accompanied his ministrations. A piece of *pagne* served as a bandage.

Biram recovered from the snake bite in a surprisingly short time. Little by little he came back from the other world where he had already set foot. Ardo poured the rest of the powder into a calabash of water. One after the other, they washed themselves in this mixture. The feet were soaked first; thus the spirits would take all reptiles out of their path.

• • •

Fary had become aware of a big monkey, almost as big as a gorilla, who had been following them since daybreak. He was often at her side, jumping on the path or in the tree branches. Several times their eyes met. He stared at her with that strange light in his eyes which she knew only too well from the way men looked at her. It made her go cold all over, so intense was the light in the animal's eyes. He groaned. From time to time he licked his lips. No one noticed him. Fary dared not talk about it. Who would believe her?

They were camping for their last night. Ardo and his companions were on watch. Mayacine was resting. Wrapped up in her

pagne, a shawl up to her eyes, Fary was stretched out near her father, looking fixedly up at the starlit sky, fighting sleep which was trying to overtake her. Something made her uneasy. She felt a presence behind her. A strange feeling ran all through her body. She turned and saw the monkey looming very large on his hind feet, his mouth open, baring his fangs and advancing towards her. She grabbed her father's gun which she secretly had learned to handle. Shivering, she was about to pull the trigger when Ardo jumped in front of her and felled the animal with his club. The beast gave a terrible cry and fell on Mayacine, who, awakening with a start, ran straight ahead, screaming. Ardo's commanding voice stopped him short. He came back, out of breath, his head hanging. The Peuls, unmoved, drank their tea.

● ● ●

It was dawn. Dusk gave way to the first rays of the new day. The sun appeared, still weak, lost in the immeasurable vastness of the sky amidst the incomparable colors of the day. The cocks crowed. The sheep bleated. From far away the sound of the pestle could be heard, the women crushing the grain, their backs arched, their arms extended, their legs wet with sweat running from their ebony bodies. Then came the call of the muezzin. Chants. Cries. Discordant noises. They were near a big village. Mayacine spoke.

"Here we are at the end of our journey. At present we are at the doors of Tiali Djiwan. I thank all of you, especially our Peul friends without whom we would be lost. The courage and vigilance of the whole group made this difficult venture possible. The Prince of Tiali shall hear about your selflessness. You, Fary, are worth a man. It is wrong to think only a man has qualities. From now on, you will be welcome on all of our expeditions."

The smile on Fary's lips was a bit forced. She did not expect that much from her father. Never, not for all the gold in the world, would she want to re-live the odyssey they had just finished.

Tiali was about five times as big as the settlement of Mboupbène. The houses were big, spacious, and solidly constructed; they reflected opulence and security. Carriages drawn by two horses went along wide, sandy, shaded streets. The women, dressed in colorful *pagnes* and *boubous,* made their way, bent from the waist, busts forward under the weight of baskets on their backs filled with food. They looked at the ragged travelers with disdain, wiggling their behinds, which were round and firm, thanks to the good food and the choice livestock Mboupbène provided.

Mayacine and his people really did not look their best. The five-day journey with all its excitement had exhausted them. Sweat made the red dust cling to their skins. Their old-fashioned clothes were in rags, showing how skinny they were. Children following them kept pointing their fingers at Fary. Their chuckling and gestures were worse than insults. Fary was the most bedraggled of the group. She kept pulling at her torn clothes, trying to cover her breasts and naked thighs, which were there for everyone to see.

They reached the pastures where the animals were to be kept. The water of a well cleaned off the dirt which had clung to them ever since they left Mboupbène. They changed their clothes. The rams, bathed and brushed, received a generous portion of straw.

The night was spent quietly in the guest huts. After sleeping in the jungle their mats put right on the floor felt like the softest cotton. Fary fell into a leaden sleep.

The next day she was particularly careful of her grooming. Her clothes were certainly shabby and miserable, but the purity of her face, the shine of her hair, and the harmony of her body were a match for any wealth.

A messenger dispatched from the palace came to inform Mayacine that the sovereign would arrive presently. The chants and tom-toms of his escort were announcing him.

Safe behind a baobab tree where the horses were tethered, Fary could observe the arrivals at leisure. A large group of men approached the pasture, some on horseback, others on foot. Beautifully garbed, they wore ample white, blue, and red shirts, held in at the waist by leather belts. Enormous billowing pants, again in red, white, and blue came to their knees and to golden yellow leather boots. They carried rifles on a shoulder strap, swords on their sides. Some wore *chechias* from which long braids escaped.

One horseman rode at the head of the group. He was riding a pure-blooded horse dressed in a brown and black blanket. The animal's steps followed the rhythms of the tom-toms. Its body was covered with precious cloths, jewels, and talismans. Its tail, dyed with henna, majestically swept from left to right, graceful as a fan in the hands of a princess. The animal's head all but disappeared under a mass of multicolored pompoms which rose and fell as the animal went ahead. An enormous parasol was held over the rider's head by another horseman who was riding at his side.

The *griots* were on foot, tom-toms at their side, sweat running down their black bodies as they forcefully called out a resplendent genealogy and most stunning exploits of their prince.

The important man alighted from his horse by stepping onto the backs of two crouching slaves. Mayacine and his sons prostrated themselves before him, kissing the ground. The Peul herdsmen were indifferent. They seemed to ignore the importance of the man and, leaning on their staffs, looked away to the horizon. Fary was grateful for her hiding place which for the moment saved her from the daily humiliations inflicted on her people. Absorbed by the goings-on and the deference and servitude of his entourage, she had hardly paid attention to the famous person himself. She now attentively looked at him. He was small, very small. A dwarf.

His enormous head disappeared under a scarlet *chechia* which had a huge gold coin in front. His face was long, his forehead prominent. His eyes were bulging under heavy, bushy eyebrows. His nose was flat, his lips large. The short legs were bowed. His arms, ridiculously short, reached to his knees. A red cape, open in the front, revealed shoulders sloping down to the waist. A pair of wide black trousers disappeared into the yellow boots, minuscule like those of a child. Her heart beating furiously, Fary, motionless, petrified with horror, looked at this apish creature, this genetic mistake, who was nothing more than an achondroplasia, a terrible case of rickets. Fear showed on her face. Suddenly, something clicked in her brain and blasted all romantic dreams. The joke was a good one! The prediction! This was Bocar Djiwan, Prince of Tiali.

"No, no!" she murmured. Her body began to shake. She felt nauseated as cramps twisted her belly. She brought up the morning mush.

The prince spoke to her father. His nasal voice was high-pitched like that of a boy.

"Mayacine Mboup, thank you for your courage and loyalty. I thank you in the name of Tiali, you and all those who helped you in your mission. I want to see them all here before me so I can congratulate them."

The herdsmen were talking in their own dialect. The rudiments of the *ouoloff* language seemed suddenly to be lost to their memories. Mayacine had to go to great efforts to get their attention. Finally they faced the little man, stiff as ramrods.

"Fary, Fary, where are you? That's my daughter," her father said in servile tones, turning his head like a top. "She accompanied us. I apologize for having gone against our customs, but she is as brave as a man. She stood up to all the dangers of the jungle."

The prince only raised his eyebrows. Seeing her father's predicament, Fary regretfully left her shielding baobab, and slowly approached. Hundreds of eyes were watching her. There were murmurs, murmurs of admiration. Her eyes met those of the prince. Here, facing her, was the ape from the jungle. She made a superhuman effort not to faint. Her emotions must have heightened her coloring. The man mistook its meaning. His own emotions were an open book; his happy smile betrayed his intentions.

"Mayacine," he said to her father, "it would be a crime to journey right back after what you have been through. The palace awaits you. You will be my guests."

The principality of Tiali for strategic reasons was built upon numerous hills, a veritable fortress which for generations had been the patrimony of its princes. The huge palace towered above one of these hills, surrounded by the others as if by a harness. One could reach it by steps carved into the rock itself. The courtyard alone was as big as Mboupbène. The sand stretched endlessly like a shiny golden carpet on which the rays of the sun threw silver spangles.

The courtyard was nearly empty when the travelers arrived. However, Fary felt that behind the imperceptibly moving curtains many eyes watched her. The travelers followed the prince. He trotted in front of them, ridiculous but alert. His small body exuded such magnetism, such force that they felt as if he were pulling them by a cord. This earthworm one could easily have squashed under one's heel held a whole people in his power. He was feared. The wise men believed him to be a reincarnation of the protecting spirit of Tiali. He headed for the large building. Slaves stretched out on the ground, offering him their backs. He kicked them with his feet, hopping like the dwarf he was.

• • •

The immense hall of the palace was fascinating, paneled and hung with rare carpets of intricate patterns. The hall all but disappeared in perfumed clouds emanating from numerous incense burners placed in each corner. It rang with the strains of the *khalam** and vibrated under the soft melodies chanted by young *griottes* accompanied by the tom-tom. Men, women, and children sat around on benches and chairs. A few sofas, occupied by women dressed in camisoles and colorful *boubous,* surrounded a huge arm-chair hung with precious silks towards which the prince propelled himself with monkey-like agility. His feet hardly touched the floor. Courtiers took off his *chechia*-crown, and bared his enormous head. He was horrible.

An old woman, skinny, with a madras headdress and wearing an impressive amount of jewelry, sat on his right. To his left were seven young women of exceptional beauty. One of them held a replica of Bocar in her arms. The prince made the introductions. Disdain flowed from the 'hawk,' the old woman with the madras headdress, the queen mother, right to the feet of the guests. The expression on her face was as clear as the water of the spring. Her mouth was pursed, eloquent. Her eyes met those of Fary, who held her gaze without flinching, holding her beautiful head high, defying her with all her being, her loveliness and youth her only trump cards.

The seven beauties were the prince's three legitimate wives and four concubines. They exchanged mocking glances, pointing

---

*a guitar

their fingers at Fary, chuckling and laughing. Fary was mad with fury. She was used to being humiliated, but not to that point. A glance from their husband made the women cower. Suddenly the chants and the music stopped. The high voice of the sovereign broke the silence.

"I am inviting Mayacine and his followers to rest in the palace to recover from their strenuous journey. They have risked their lives to bring us our sheep. They shall be our guests. The west building is reserved for Mayacine and his men. The east wing is for his daughter."

All eyes fell on Fary. The irony of those looks and the insistence of the prince's alarmed her. She guessed. Later she was to find out that the east wing regularly received young virgins whose parents offered them to the prince. She became afraid. She could not suppress a sob which made her father uneasy. He too had guessed. Regrets tortured him. Why had he been so weak and given in to his daughter? Not true, she had not even asked to go. But her eagerness and her interest in all that concerned the expedition, even to the selection of the sheep, her curiosity about the principality of Tiali had all contributed to making him lose his head. He could not have foreseen the prince's reaction. Suddenly he discovered that instead of his child, there was a woman before him, beautiful and exciting, of a beauty that bites like pepper and makes every man want to possess her.

"*Astakhfirla* I repent, Lord, I repent," he murmured, ashamed of the incestuous thoughts that had come over him for a moment. The appearance of an uncountable number of dishes, beef, lamb, chicken, roasted guinea fowl, millet, cous-cous, calabashes of honey, of mush topped with big chunks of heavy cream took his mind off his worries. His mouth began to water. He opened his eyes wide, swallowed a few times. For the first time in his life he was facing such a feast, such an assortment of food.

Legs of lamb, duck, gourds full of ginger beer, red *bissap,* and sorrel juice were in abundance. Mayacine relegated the thought of the east wing and its virgins to a far corner of his mind. He ate, devoured, stuffed himself. Succulent pieces of meat disappeared, washed down with gulps of ginger beer interspersed with loud belches. Biram and Tior wolfed down the fresh meat like young animals. Their faces smeared with fat, they grimaced like monkeys.

Making herself small in a corner, Fary watched with disdain. The shepherds sipped their tea, their legs crossed, ostentatiously turning their backs to all this food.

The prince kept emptying small flasks of *rikless,* a mint-flavored alcoholic drink, or dipping into the calabashes of mead near him.

Mayacine lifted his head and met his daughter's gaze. He asked to be taken to the west wing.

• • •

Fary was taken to the east wing by a shrewd-looking old woman who had the air of a procuress. Her room was perfumed with incense. The open bed was covered with immaculate white sheets. The old woman unlocked some trunks, took out robes, unfolded *boubous* and luxurious cloths which for a moment dazzled Fary. The old crone put some perfumes at Fary's feet and with a leering smile that showed her toothless gums, wished Fary a good night, closing the door gently behind her.

After having made sure that the old woman was gone, really gone, Fary left the room on tiptoe and ran over to the west wing. She ran blindly along the maze of unknown corridors, going from door to door until she suddenly happened upon Tior, doubled up in cramps and sobbing. The unaccustomed riches of the meal were making him ill. Then the hiccups and streams of vomit came from his throat, spilling to the floor. He lifted his head and saw his sister.

"Where do you come from, Fary?"

"Never mind. Take me to father and be quick about it."

After turning a few corners in the corridor, Tior gently opened a door. A small oil lamp cast a soft light over the room. Mayacine was praying. His hands towards heaven, he asked the Lord for forgiveness, to have mercy on the sins his daughter was about to commit, all through his fault. He prayed with fervor, tears streaming from his eyes. It was the first time in her life Fary had witnessed such a spectacle.

Mayacine knew what his daughter could expect. All his principles were opposed, but what could he do against the prince? He felt a presence, turned around and saw his daughter. Aloud he thanked Allah and locked the door with a double turn of the key. Fary and her father went to sleep.

• • •

They spent five days in the palace, five days without incident. The prince ignored Fary's presence.

On the day of their departure he gave them a royal escort and showered them with presents.

On the way home Mayacine took his daughter aside and said, "Fary, because of the respect you owe me as your father, I am asking you for complete silence on what almost happened between the Prince of Tiali and you. He is a powerful man, venerated and respected despite his ugliness. He did not expect such an insult as a refusal by you, a *griotte*, a woman of caste and an untouchable, when the most beautiful and highest born young girls are offered to him every day. I have the presentiment that he has a surprise in store for us. This story must under no circumstances get around. Bocar has many complexes and his reactions cannot be anticipated. Swear."

She raised her hand and said, "I swear."

Fary was happy to be reunited with her friend Coura and told her about their journey in the greatest detail, omitting, however, all that concerned Bocar.

Coura listened avidly, doubled up with laughter, but had difficulty believing all she heard.

"You ought to believe me when I tell you you are beautiful, Fary. You see, even monkeys fall victim to your beauty." And again she started laughing.

"Don't laugh like a madwoman. Tell me what's been happening in my absence."

"Nothing, really, except for the way your awful Gana acted. He would like to have beaten me because I couldn't stop you from making this journey which everyone here considers a folly. He thought that, as your best friend, I should have been able to dissuade you from going. If you act in such a cavalier fashion, you may lose him. He certainly won't let you lead him around by the nose as you have a habit of doing."

"We shall see. Bigger and more powerful people have done my bidding, why not Gana? But what's new with you?"

"I have an acceptable suitor, not too old, two wives, in his forties, handsome, slightly greying, a good future."

"Do I know him?"

"Do you ever!" she said mockingly. Then, without further enlightening Fary, she asked to accompany her to her aunt Sokhna's house. She was going to consult the cowrie shells to prepare to defend herself in the future from her co-wives, who would not fail to go on the warpath, trying to prevent an intruder's joining the household.

They were only a few steps from Sokhna's house when the galloping of a horse and rider caught their attention. Quickly they hid behind a fence.

It was Mayoro. He was dressed like a prince. His horse was loaded with enormous bundles. His particular scent tickled their noses and throats. It was musky like Zeuma's perfumes. He dismounted and went into his ladyfriend's house, closing the door behind him.

• • •

Fary and Coura were now alone. Dusk was approaching. The sun, like a ball of fire, disappeared on the horizon of the streaked western sky. It was the propitious hours for the *djins,* the spirits who, most often in the form of winds, wrought evil on people.

Fary pulled Coura by the hand. She resisted a little, then followed. They hid behind the house, poked an opening into the wall, and waited. Coura kept moving and repeating, "Let's go. It's late." This did not stop her from craning her neck in order not to miss anything going on in the house.

As Fary and Coura watched, the man put down his bundles and stretched out on the bed. Sokhna greeted him with a deep curtsy.

"What a lovely perfume, uncle, is it new?"

The man pulled a vial from his pocket and sprinkled some perfume on his paramour. Fary inhaled a cloud of fragrance that nearly choked her. Sokhna did not seem to mind the powerful scent. She lifted the bottle to her nose and smelled it. Then she pulled off the man's boots, washed his feet, dried them gently, and massaged them.

"You are worn out, uncle. Your journey was long and tedious. Your feet must really have suffered." She helped him to undress.

Coura stood on tiptoes now. Her moist hand squeezed Fary's.

The man stretched out on the bed. The woman covered him with *pagnes* so steeped in incense that the pleasant odor reached the two girls' lookout post.

The man hardly spoke. Expert hands travelled over his body and sometimes caused him to sigh. He raised himself on his elbow, lit his pipe, and exhaled one puff. For the first time in his turbulent existence he was really worried. The woman's expert caresses elicited no response from his body. Sokhna was perturbed.

"Uncle, what is wrong with you today? Are you ill? Do you have any worries?"

"Hm," was his only answer.

"How is your prince? Is everything well with him?"

"Hm!" Another sound.

"Still a wolf?"

"Hm!"

"But, what is the matter with you today? You seem very strange. I can sense that you are hiding something from me. I can tell by just looking at you." She walked away from him.

Slowly her bewitching *betion,* a small white *pagne* with black stripes, lifted to reveal long legs and a scarlet garter of charms around the knee. A few strands of white pearls appeared briefly, clicking suggestively. A hand, as if inadvertently, gratified the man with a brief caress. Her blouse was open. A sleeve came down. A firm breast held its nipple out to Mayoro. His eyes became glazed.

He looked at Sokhna full of lust. His Adam's apple rose and fell. She now excited him in an inexplicable way. Ensconsed in the depths of the soft bed, he panted like a long-distance runner. The blouse went back in place, the *pagne* fell, the sleeve went up. The woman looked lasciviously at the man, hummed a little tune, and tended the fire which filled the room with a wonderful fragrance.

"I'm listening to you, uncle. When something is wrong, it is better to bring it out in the open. What is it you have to tell me?"

"Will you swear by your father's belt that this will be between just us two and really just us two?"

"You insult me. This is something new. Since when have you made me swear? If you no longer trust me, then your place is no longer here."

The man got very close to the woman he desired and, looking at her cleavage, whispered.

Coura chose this very moment to divert Fary's attention.

"Fary, if you don't want to leave, *I* am going. It's getting late. My parents will worry."

"Go ahead, Coura. I'll follow. I am going to wait a little longer."

"Your curiosity will be your undoing."

"No matter what happens, I am going to find out."

It seemed as if Mayoro had only waited for Coura to leave. He started to talk at last.

"Do you know the daughters of Mayacine Mboup?"

"Yes. Incidentally, the eldest accompanied her father to Tiali. Mayacine is mad to involve a girl in such an adventure."

"He is mad indeed, and the adventure was not the jungle but Bocar Djiwan Malick, Prince of Tiali."

"What? Did he succumb to the girl's charms?"

"What a woman! You guessed it."

Sokhna seemed preoccupied. She twisted and twisted her *pagne*.

Mayoro continued, "An extraordinary thing happened. For the first time in his life, Bocar Malick was ridiculed by a woman and by what kind of a woman? A *griotte,* a woman of caste, an untouchable. This Fary refused to give herself to him. To insult the prince of Tiali in such a fashion really takes a lot of courage."

"That's true. Fary has a lot of spirit. She is different from the faint-hearted girls of her generation who are held back by their outdated, spineless upbringing. Somebody else would have been an easier mark."

"To turn down the prince of Tiali!" Mayoro intoned like a recurring theme.

"And you find that abnormal? Why should she make him a present of her honor?"

"If he had wanted to, he could have taken her by force. For what reason does she go unpunished? That is the real mystery. Her impertinence has exceeded all limits. Call it what you like; love, passion, falling for her. Of one thing I am certain. He is mad. He wants her for his wife, but one big problem remains. His worthy mother, high and mighty as she is, despises our race. She will never accept such a misalliance, even if her own ancestors have married *griottes.*"

"She seems to forget how misshapen her son is. If he were not a crowned head, who would want a monster like him?"

"This monster, as you say, has the most beautiful collection of women I know. It's hardly choice that he lacks. This Fary is far from possessing their beauty, even though she is attractive and bright."

"That is just why she is special. She is above them because she has class, an aura—presence, charm, and pride. Men do not like easy conquests. I am sure that this refusal to belong to your prince is undoubtedly the first rejection in his life and must have influenced his decision to make her his wife. You may be sure he will get his way in spite of his mother."

"I should be surprised. For this man who knows no pity, who is hard, is always most reluctant to rebel against his mother. She has a diabolical influence over him. Bocar has confided in me, his *beuk-nek*. I saw how tormented and unhappy he was. It took some doing, but with patience and ruses I managed to have him confide in me. Now he leaves everything in my hands. It's up to me, or rather up to the two of us, to resolve the problem."

A wide smile appeared on Sokhna's face.

"Still more reason to glorify my ancestors. They are infallible. First thing tomorrow I will bring them the blood of a sacrificed white lamb, soured milk, and cola nuts. It has been exactly three years to the day when I predicted to Fary Mboup, who with my niece Coura, had come to consult me, that she would marry a prince, small, black, and ugly, but rich. I did not quite expect that she would land as big a fish as the prince of Tiali."

Mayoro jumped up in bed as if bitten by a serpent.

"Why didn't you say so right away? Do consult your cowries again."

She pulled her frame from under her bed, threw her cowries, and said, "What difficulties, intrigues, plots and surprises surround this union! However, it will take place. Look. These two cowries in the middle symbolize marriage, the marriage of a young girl to a highly-placed person. The remaining ninety-eight cowries show the various situations which will undeniably arise as soon as this union is talked about. *Kilifas,* people of high rank, men and women of all ages and all social classes will intervene. But all their *pekhes*, their machinations will have no effect. This marriage, though I don't know when or how, will surely take place. However, there is one thing that worries me. What was Fary's reaction when she saw Bocar?"

"I believe I was the only one who observed her when they turned over the sheep. She had hidden behind a tree, where, at one point, she started to vomit. Then she nearly fainted when her father presented her to the prince.

"Do you think she will accept this monster for a husband despite his titles and his money?" Mayoro asked.

"You are asking me too much. I know that at the moment she is in love with Gana Mboup, the son of Baye Daour, the deaf man. Gana is young and handsome, no comparison with that dwarf. But, all things considered, she would be wrong to refuse this chance. A monkey covered with gold is better than a naked peacock."

"That is your opinion, Sokhna, but surely not hers. Again, how can we solve this problem?"

"I think we should consult Tierno, my mother's cousin. You know him. He excels in unraveling such mysteries. More than once has he saved us."

And without any superfluous preliminaries, Mayoro threw her down on the bed.

Fary left.

• • •

Serigne Tierno was the reigning *marabout* of Ndiom, a small settlement halfway between the principality of Tiali and the village of Mboupbène. His family had held that position for generations. However, his power was waning. A competitor who had established himself near Tiali awed everyone by the accuracy of his predictions and the success of his treatments. Thus, the whole population, seeking something new, flocked to his hut.

Facing east, his arms lifted to heaven, Tierno deferentially spoke to God:

> *Lord, merciful and compassionate*
> *Lord of heaven and earth*
> *Lord over life and death,*
> *Lord of the spirits and of men,*
> *Lord of all riches. I implore you.*
> *Humble is your servant who reaches out to you*
> *Humble is the one who asks but the smallest drop*
> *of the immeasurable ocean of your wealth,*
> *Lord . . . . .*

The sound of steps in the silence of the dawn put an end to Tierno's invocations. He took his prayer beads and listened. The sounds came closer. A ray of hope came to him; he could smell an important piece of business, for usually only important people chose this discreet hour of the day to come for a consultation.

He almost jumped with joy when he recognized the voice of Mayoro, the confidant of the bigwigs of Tiali. The chance of earning a lot of money cheered him. He eagerly went inside, preceeding Mayoro. The greetings, contrary to the custom, were brief.

"Is it only peace which brings you so early in the morning?"

"Only a serious problem insoluble to my mind is the reason for my presence."

"May one know your problem? Nothing resists the divine

mercy. God has given us all powers except life and resurrection. Those are his alone. He gives life and he takes it away according to his will. Speak without fear, I am listening."

"My intuition was not wrong. You are the one we need."

"Who is we?"

"The prince of Tiali and I."

The *marabout* kept crossing and uncrossing his legs.

"I was right to have sought you out, for without doubt your ancestors have passed on to you their immense knowledge which until now has been unsurpassed in our region."

Tierno's answer betrayed his irritation, for he was eager to know the motive for the visit. Prince Bocar was the most coveted client of all *marabouts* in the territory.

"Mayoro, come to the point. Explain clearly what brought you here. There is not much time. I am expecting advice seekers any minute."

"Prince Bocar Djiwan Malick has asked me to find him a competent man able to resolve a difficult problem. He does not know that I am here. This visit is on my initiative only. He is in love with a young girl."

Tierno, bent over his beads, nodded his head.

"She is a *griotte*." Staring at Mayoro, he raised his head.

"He wants to make her his fourth wife. His mother will oppose it with all her might."

Tierno's eyes went wide and became as round as saucers.

"The object of my visit is to ask you to use your influence with the queen mother, make her silent as the grave, docile as a lamb, so that henceforth she approves of everything her son does, now, and in the future. Her despotism has caused many incidents in Tiali, but her son venerates her."

Tierno listened, nodding his head and silently fingering his prayer beads. From time to time he turned around circumspectly, stroking his beard, as impassive as a marble statue. Finally, he took a shallow basket and filled it with sand. With his fingers he poked holes aligned in even and uneven pairs and recited incantations. He wiped them out. He traced them a second time, wiped them out once more.

Then he squinted, put his chin in his hand, and concluded. "Ahem! Yes! This union could be brought about. It will take an enormous amount of work. Three days of isolation in the jungle in our family sanctuary accompanied by prayers, sacrifices, risks, and expenses. I will take them upon myself. Tomorrow I will exile myself. I will do everything to solve this entanglement, only the second of its kind in my long life."

"At present, master, all is in your hands."

"Unless I am mistaken, it is Sunday. Come to see me next Thursday after evening prayers. Let us figure the cost."

He took up his basket again, poked his holes in the sand, retraced them, let his fingers wander about as in a game of checkers, murmured his incantations, concluding, "A young cow who is calfing for the first time, three white rams, three sheep of the same color, a bull, seven *pagnes*, seven calabashes of soured milk, seven of millet, seven of peanuts, seven of *niebe* beans, three times seven gold pieces, three times seven silver pieces."

Mayoro's surprise was without equal. This was the first time since he had recourse to such services that he had been presented with such a bill. A fortune! The coffers of Tiali would be emptied. Was this Fary worth such a fortune? Little did his opinion matter. He had only to carry out orders.

"Just make sure this marriage takes place," Bocar had told him. "At what price?" he now asked himself. New taxes on the harvest, new taxes on the herds would surely be imposed in Mboupbène without delay.

The moonless sky disappeared, hidden by the shadows whose immense black mantle covered the town. The coach advanced in the opaque darkness on jumbled lanes, guided by clever horses trained for these roads and journeys in the night. At length the coach came to a halt.

A woman alighted, furtively glancing around, then went towards Serigne Tierno's hut. Three sharp knocks and the door opened. After the customary salutations, the *marabout* went back to his prayer rug and with his finger pointed to a mat, invited the woman to sit down. A few more rows of his prayer beads allowed him to observe his guest at leisure. It was the queen mother, the dowager, the mother of the prince of Tiali, the most powerful person in the principality. She was nervous and her right hand fidgeted with her *pagne*.

Tierno did not know how to address her. Frightened by the ambiguous situation her visit put him in, he asked in a trembling voice, "What guides your steps to me so early in the morning and from so far away? Is it only peace?"

"I have to return to Tiali immediately, before daybreak," she answered in a biting voice. "My escort is waiting. I need not ask you to keep my visit a secret. Discretion has always been one of your ancestors' numerous qualities, which explains why our family has been attached to yours for generations. Anxiety alone has guided my steps here. I have had exactly the same nightmare as ten years ago, the night before my husband died. I saw the same scene again with extraordinary clarity. A woman with a very dark complexion, walking on her toes, approached my son and offered him a bloody leg of lamb, just as the woman in the dream did to his father ten years ago. The dream was strangely clear and precise. The woman's features are etched in my memory. Tall and black, a scar at the corner of her mouth."

Tierno, who had regained his composure, looked at the ceiling of his hut, clicking his beads, and said in a tone full of authority, almost aggressively, "Will you tell me your dream once more so that I can consult the Holy Books?"

Once again she told him her story. Stripped of her conceit and her mantle of the despot, she was just another mother trembling for the future of her son.

Tierno consulted a book, lifted his head, and said seriously, "Indeed, in a dream meat and blood symbolize misfortune, even death. There is a woman in your house who carries the seal of fatality, the *gaffe*. She is black, young, tall, and slim and walks on tiptoe. Do you know who she is?"

"No," she answered after a few moments.

"She is very close to you. Do you not see her?"

"No."

"How many wives does your son have?"

"Three."

"Will you describe them for me?"

"The first one is small, stout, of light complexion, with tattooed lips. The second is of medium height, not very black, slim, slim," she repeated herself. "But she has no scar. The third is tall. Slim." She started to breathe hard. "She has a scar at the corner of the lips." She was perspiring. "Yes, yes, it is true. She walks on her toes." Her voice became toneless. "It is she who has the *gaffe*." She cried out as if demented, "How could I have been so blind?"

"It is not given to all of us to solve the mysteries."

"Yes. That is why I came to you. I have absolute confidence in your family's vision. I came to tell you about the dream in great haste so we could conjure fate by prayer before it is too late."

"It is a difficult task—sacrifices, expenses, isolating myself in our sanctuary in the heart of the jungle. I will devote myself to your cause body and soul. The steps which brought you here shall not have been in vain. But I must ask you to keep absolutely silent. This must remain strictly between the two of us. You must show no hostility towards the third wife. Nothing of what you fear will come to pass if God does not take the spiritual heritage of my ancestors away from my memory. Come back Friday at the same hour."

"And the cost?" the woman asked.

Tierno took a board, put it on his knees, dipped his feather into the ink, and started to draw. After making several mysterious signs he announced the bill: "One cow, one bull, three white rams. Three white sheep. Seven white chickens. Seven red roosters. A donkey. A female donkey. A horse. A brood mare. Seven times seven gold pieces."

Tierno seemed determined to reconstitute his family's patrimony all at once, especially its renowned livestock: race horses, working donkeys, prize rams who had been the winners at fairs, but ended up in the pastures of Tiali.

● ● ●

When the woman had left, Tierno called his two wives, one after the other. His third wife had not yet joined his household, but was still living with her parents in Mboupbène.

"Here is the situation," he told his first wife. "I am called upon to accomplish extremely serious work in the darkest secrecy. I know you are discreet. Your tongue doesn't play tricks on you like that of the other one. For three days I must remain sequestered in the isolation hut behind the slaughter house. If visitors ask for me, tell them that I am far away on a journey visiting a sick relative. I must not be disturbed for any reason. The communion with the spirits demands darkness and silence. Any unforeseen disturbance could cause death or madness.

"On the first and second day you will discreetly bring my meals before the last prayer. Make some detours to mislead people. No one must see you enter the hut."

Then it was the second wife's turn. "Several times I have had to deplore the lack of discretion of your co-wife concerning certain subjects we were the only ones to speak of in bed," he told her. "I would not like it if it were the same with you. I have an important

task to accomplish for the prince of Tiali and it must be done with the greatest secrecy. To avoid being disturbed I will stay in the isolation house for three days. You will bring me the morning mush at dawn. Be cautious and avoid encounters. Only cross the doorstep of the hut if you are sure you have not been seen. If you have any doubts, go back home and I'll do without the meal. As far as anyone knows, even the children, I have gone on a journey."

Late in the night, when all of his children slept soundly, Tierno, the great *marabout* of Ndiom, with his gift of seeming to be everywhere at once, moved into his place of meditation.

Tierno's prayers were interminable at this late hour of the night. His incantations defied all spiritual science. His long string of prayer beads clicked dully with the sound of large pestles pounding in mortars. An enormous turban was wound around his head. His starched *boubou* made a rasping sound everytime he moved. A special mystery seemed to surround him. Everything about him, even his clothing, was designed to intimidate the already tormented queen mother. She seemed to come out of a dream when the *marabout's* grave voice reached her.

"The *khalwa,* the retreat has been especially difficult. I have come back from our family's sanctuary in the heart of the jungle where for three days and three nights I had to fight all sorts of evil spirits. It is a serious problem, very serious. My life was in danger several times. If it had been for anyone but you, I would have given up, but I could not idly stand by and watch the misfortune that threatens our prince. The problem is very complicated. Listen well. Pay attention. It is extremely important.

"I had a first revelation. A strong and indestructible love binds your son to the wife whom destiny chose for him. They are bound for all eternity. The hand of the mortals cannot undo what God has joined together even before we were born.

"After much searching, after numerous and difficult communications with the spirits of my ancestors, the spirits have indicated a solution: the *todieule.* This means killing the evil at its source, to prevent its spreading, to kill it at its very roots.

"The *todieule* took me a whole day and night of work, of meditation, of concentration, of battle with the terrible spirit which has been living in this woman since her birth. The solution is marriage. The prince must marry a fourth wife."

After a long sigh the queen mother answered, "I agree with

you. His father had four when he was his age."

"There are stipulations, requirements, *tektels* concerning his future wife. She was shown to me as clearly as I see the cowrie shells in this basket. I saw her as clearly as I am seeing you."

"Who is she? Who? Who?"

Deep silence reigned in the hut. His head lowered, as rigid as a marble statue, the pitiless Tierno, by his silence, even indifference, added to the fear in the old woman's heart.

"Who?" repeated the woman gripped by the greatest anguish. Her flabby cheeks were trembling, her fleshless hands held her *pagne* like the claws of a vulture.

Tierno looked up at last at the woman and in a grave voice said, "A *griotte* from Mboupbêne. Fary Mboup, daughter of Mayacine and Lala Mboup, is the only one who can save your son."

"No! No!" she cried out like a wounded animal and fell to the floor. Tierno rushed to her, throwing water on her face. She was as limp as a corpse. He took off his *boubou* which hindered his movements. With shaking hands he slapped her face, shook the lifeless body, massaged her chest. She still did not respond. Tierno, undone, knelt to pray.

"Help me, my God. Don't let her die here. Don't take her life in my house. I should be done for. I promise my God to burn a ram, a bull. I promise to recite the whole Koran from now on, to give alms, to obey your commandments. I promise . . ." He promised without end.

Then he sprinkled different essences on the woman, one of which gave off a strong odor of ammonia. The queen mother sneezed. Little by little she regained consciousness. She remained prostrate for a long time. Full of a heavy, piercing pain, her voice rose in the silence of the room.

"I have been right to despise her, this *griotte,* more than any other of her race. Her diabolical beauty has bewitched my son. From the moment I first saw her, I distrusted her. She is an ambitious girl who knows no shame. An uneducated, brazen girl who dared not to flinch when I looked at her, me, whose look has been the spine of many princes. She came to trouble my son, to provoke him. She pursued him under his very roof. Her sorcery got the better of him. Should I destroy the principles which have guided us for generations? Could I soil my posterity? Could my family honor have a blotch which can never be erased? Death, yes, death to Bocar!"

"Yes, death, death for Bocar," repeated Tierno.

"No, not the death of my only son, this son who for all of you is nothing but a monster."

"*Asbomalah!* Repent. Don't perjure yourself. What a terrible misconception. For those of us who can see farther than their noses, your son is the fruit of God's will, of Him who once again has shown that He alone is judge and sovereign. He gave your son the appearance He chose. Despite his appearance, your son is feared and respected and leads a whole people."

In an emotional voice the queen continued, "This son I had so desired, this monster which I cherish, this only child I had such trouble carrying in my being! Dishonor, ridicule, rather than his death. No, No, better death than shame!"

She could not decide what her feelings were in the painful turmoil which engulfed her with the violence of a flood at the equinox.

Then, after some more exchanges with Tierno, she asked him, "Can't you find a solution other than marriage, Serigne?"

"No, my ancestors speak only once. It's Fary or death." Ostentatiously he turned his back to her.

Little by little the starlit night gave way to the fluorescent clarity of dawn. The outlines of the huts could be seen far away against a sky filled with gigantic, milky-white layers of clouds whose contours were nebulous, sometimes non-existent. A slight breeze went through the trees, picked the dewdrops from their leaves and scattered them on the ground in various weird designs.

Falla and Yande, Bocar's second and third wives, whose friendship was based only on their coalition against Deguène, the first wife and the prince's favorite, were about to visit their aunt-in-law whose property was a mile from the palace.

"What do you think of Bocar?" Falla asked.

"In what regard?"

"Don't play the innocent. You know very well what I am talking about."

"To be frank, I don't know."

"Did you notice the sudden change in him? He is like a chameleon. He gets angry about nothing. He has become as irritable as a caged lion. The food is too salty. His clothes are never clean enough. The children get on his nerves. He is just the opposite of what he used to be. All day long I hear nothing but complaints. For months now I share the bed of a eunuch. He is as cold as a slug."

"To tell the truth, I have noticed the same thing ever since the herd of sheep arrived three years ago. A witch doctor I consulted gave me a magic powder whose only effect was a name he mumbles in his sleep, Fary or Farly. Do you remember a young *griotte* who was with the sheep-herders? She was beautiful and arrogant, but so poor it made our beggars look rich. But her beauty was exceptional. I think that she is the one. I am even sure of it, for he kept looking at her all the time. Then the group was staying at the palace and that was something new. The east wing had been given to the girl."

"A *griotte?* Impossible. She won't stand a chance. For once the queen mother will be on our side. She would never accept such a misalliance. And what does the Princess Deguène think of all of this?"

"Try and find out. She barely gives me the time of day. Her station as first wife gives her rights which my lady wears like a crown on her head. She must suffer as much as we do, but would rather die than admit it. Out of prudence we will go to Serigne Tierno to secure our positions."

"You can go by yourself. It's not to die for love that I sacrificed my youth, my beauty, and the handsome princes who courted me before I married this monster. If he has no respect for our noble blood, I shall leave him without regrets."

"Falla, when the time comes, you will go with me. How do you think you can get away from Bocar? Instead of listening to your pride, which will be your downfall, you will accompany me to Tierno's."

It was the feast day of Tiali. The same ritual as in previous years was being observed. The people of Tiali went from door to door to wish their neighbors a happy holiday and to ask forgiveness for their sins which as in any community were manifold. Bocar was no exception to this rule. He prostrated himself before his mother who with a quavering voice praised her son.

"I forgive you, son. Forgive me, son. You have never sinned against me. You have always been submissive. You are aware of the importance to your well-being, of the happiness resulting from your parents' blessing. I bestow it upon you. Try and preserve it until death. It is your only protection in this world.

"It is time that you thought of taking a fourth wife. I take advantage of this day, blessed among all others, to speak of it. Life is full of dangers. Your life would be in peril if you did not respect certain predictions. I had a great deal of trouble bringing you into this world and I don't want to lose you for any reason whatsoever. I cannot tell you more. I have not always been kind to you. I have been hard and demanding, but it was always for your own good."

The prince was puzzled. What was she trying to get at? Why did she speak to him in such a calm voice with no sign of an impending storm? It was not like her to use so many preambles without getting to the point directly.

He watched her and had trouble recognizing his mother in this woman who looked tired and worn, but was serene, quite the opposite of the haughty and bitter dowager he was used to.

"There it is. We cannot always do things in life the way we would choose. For reasons which I cannot explain to you, except that they are for your security, I am willing to ignore the conventions, to violate our customs and to leave ourselves open to the criticism of our race, and to ask you one more time to follow my wishes. Your fourth wife shall be a *griotte*. I have already chosen her. Her name is Fary Mboup. She is from the village of Mboupbène."

With a superhuman effort she stifled her sobs. With a wave of the hand she dismissed her son.

"Mother, I have never dared to question the wisdom of your decisions. May lightning strike me if I should be so bold as to do so now. May your will be done."

"May God keep you, my son."

A long time had passed since the day when Fary witnessed the conversation between the two lovers. She had been late getting home where her mother had waited up for her. What an irony of fate for Coura to have left just when Mayoro had finally deigned to open his mouth. To be the wife of the prince of Tiali, would that not be the answer to all her problems?

"Yes," one voice told her. "Here is the answer to your problems." "No," said another. "Your love of perfection would make this union impossible. To be the wife of a monster, a dwarf, to stand this earthworm, his embraces, his face, his eyes, to see him when you wake up in the morning, to carry his child, cradle a dwarf in your arms . . . what hell!"

"No! No!" she answered this unseen voice which persecuted her right into her sleep. A terrible fever accompanied her nightmares, and pain tortured her day and night.

Her mother, far from suspecting the truth, believed her to be bewitched. Fary had difficulties recovering from her illness, undoubtedly the longest and most severe in her life.

When the *marabouts* in the area could not help her, Fary's parents scraped together their last resources for a visit to Serigne Tierno, who, because of his high prices, was the last one on their list.

They arrived well before daybreak. Tierno was finishing his devotions. Mayacine and Lala, respectful and fearful, crouched in a corner of the hut. The prayers, silent when they arrived, became progressively louder and more deafening. Fary watched him. Disregarding the special concentration usually accorded any prayer, Tierno studied these unknown visitors carefully. He spit on his hands, put them to his face, his head, his body, punctuating his gestures with an "amen" which the parents repeated like parrots. He annointed his face and arms with three liquids contained in three different vials, put on his charms, greeted the visitors, and inquired about the object of their visit.

Mayacine approached him on hands and knees and said in a barely audible voice, "Only worry has led us to you. We want to help our daughter who has been ill for a long time."

Tierno gave the patient a glance. Not at all intimidated, Fary looked at him full of curiosity, unlike her parents whose bent heads almost touched the floor.

"What is she suffering from?"

"She is possessed. She cries, especially at night. She, who used to be so expansive, no longer speaks. She hardly eats and she often cries without reason."

"What does she say when she cries out?"

"It is rather mixed up, but the word 'no' is often on her lips."

"*No*. Why 'no'? To whom does she say 'no'?"

"That is what we would like to know, Serigne."

"If it pleases God, you will know." He raised his *boubou*, dipped his hand into a calabash filled with water where horns, iron rings, bronze rings, bird beaks, feathers, and the feet of roosters were piled up. After some oracular mutterings, he asked the patient's name.

"Fary Mboup, daughter of Mayacine and Lala Mboup."

It was as if a serpent had bitten Tierno's hand. He jerked it out of the calabash. He lost his composure. He looked at Fary imperiously. She was obviously the only one who had witnessed his emotion. She looked at Tierno with defiance. After some moments of silence, he spoke to Mayacine.

"Let the patient come closer."

Pulled by her father's strong hand, Fary complied.

"Let her bend over the calabash."

Not at all terrified, as most patients would be at this point, Fary did obediently what she was asked. Tierno had his wet hand on Fary's neck and again started his incantations. After some minutes he asked Mayacine and his wife to leave the room. He found himself alone with Fary.

"We are alone now, my child. Have confidence. Tell me what torments you." She kept silent.

"Speak. We are without witnesses. Our conversation will never go beyond this room."

Still no answer.

"What are you afraid of?"

"Didn't you hear my parents? I am bewitched."

The *marabout* laughed. "Your parents think so, but you and I know you are not bewitched."

"Why would I be here?"

"Because of what troubles you, what you keep locked in your heart that frightens you. It may be a mystery for others, but it is clear to me. I will find the answer easily with or without your help. I am asking myself if I have not already found it."

Not at all impressed, she gave the man an inscrutable look. Her eyes were insolent as she defied him with a mocking smile.

"Let's see now," he said bitterly, "the principality of Tiali wouldn't have anything to do with your illness?"

Fary was visibly troubled. She began to tremble uncontrollably and to laugh hysterically.

"No! No!" she repeated. "Never."

"Calm yourself, my child. Calm down, little girl. We surely have a lot to talk about. I have all the time in the world. Tell me everything from the beginning to the end."

On their way back from the market Fary and Coura sat down to rest under Mboupbène's great mango tree.

"This is a chance to talk to you I have been awaiting a long time, Fary."

"What about, Coura?"

"About the way you have changed, about whatever it is that torments you. I know you well enough to notice that you are hiding something from me. You are only a shadow of your former self. And if you want me to put it more pointedly, I have noticed a difference ever since you came back from Tiali.

"You seemed very unhappy for a little while, but after two months you were yourself again. Then after our visit to Sokhna, you seemed to have the same symptoms all over again. What happened? What did you find out? I recall leaving you just when Uncle Mayoro was about to speak.

"Is it about your parents? You are not obliged to tell me your secrets. I am asking out of friendship and compassion. I feel that you want to confide in me, but something is holding you back. Is it so serious then?"

Fary's shoulders rose as sobs shook her whole body. Her tears ran like a fountain.

"Excuse me. Forgive me if I have made a mistake. I would never have asked if I had doubted our friendship or affection for each other." She made ready to go, extremely embarrassed. Fary held Coura by her *pagne*.

"Do you remember Sokhna's prediction three and a half years ago?"

"That you were going to be a princess?"

"It is about to come true."

Coura beamed. She looked at the crown which in her imagination already encircled her friend's head.

"But with whom?"

"With a monster, a dwarf, a gargoyle."

Coura lifted her calabash and hurled it into the air. It fell and broke with a dull thud, food flying in all directions.

"Is this a story or a joke? If it is, it's in very bad taste."

"It is strictly the truth. Neither you nor I had ever seen the prince of Tiali. He is tremendously rich, but he is a dwarf."

Coura looked at her friend as if seeing her for the first time.

"Refuse this marriage. Nothing forces you. An ugly man, yes, but not a dwarf. As I know you, you could never live with him even if he gave you all the gold in the world. Think of the utter hell you would live in."

"That is what I have told myself hundreds of times and what I haven't stopped repeating to myself. However, there is a much more important aspect that dominates my personal feelings and seems stronger than my revulsion.

"I am not an offering to be immolated, nor do I pretend to be a savior, but I am deeply convinced that this marriage would be one half of the scissors which will cut the chains of slavery and end the humiliation of my race."

"*Daga boumou diam?* To cut the chains of slavery? Never will you accomplish that. How can you expect through a simple marriage to destroy the principles existing for generations, anchored in our traditions, as unmovable as the sky above which has been there over our heads since the dawn of creation?

"You are dreaming, my friend. Don't sacrifice your life for day-dreams. Gana loves you. He is handsome. He will be rich. His uncle will give him a dowry for your wedding. Marry him; your children will be as beautiful as angels."

"This time, Coura, we are not speaking the same language. Our roads lead us apart. You can't understand. It is not ambition that guides my steps, nor frustration, nor hope for Utopia. Bocar's wealth does not corrupt me. My ideal is something else completely. My goal is to fight inequality for a better future for my people."

"Fary, come back to earth. Did you forget that horrible scene we had to witness: the whipping of your uncle Ibra and his children? The desecration of his mother's tomb? And why? For having disobeyed the powers which rule us.

"And you, poor girl, want to oppose them? A young woman, still almost a child, empty-handed, trying to oppose centuries of tradition. I strongly doubt that you could succeed."

"You still don't understand, my friend. But you should know this: I will accept this marriage. It is my very own uncle and his family who have brought me to this decision. Until my death shall I remember the humiliation, this most shameful act inflicted upon my abject race. I feel it is my duty to fight it."

"If this is your decision, may God help you. You are like my sister. Your happiness is mine. If you think you can find it with the prince of Tiali, you have my blessing."

"I am grateful, Coura. When the time comes, I will call on you for help."

"You can count on me."

Silently the two friends returned to the village.

● ● ●

Mayacine, surrounded by his children, was making mats for the enclosure around the house. Tior was always conspicuous by his absence during common enterprises which united the rest of the family.

He was in the forest with some of the neighborhood children killing birds with slingshots, and eating the birds on the spot after roasting them over a wood fire.

They were eating a dessert of papayas stolen in the neighboring fields when Tior and the children were suddenly aware of the sound of voices coming from the far side of a thicket.

"Should we warn Mayacine?"

"No, the prince did not instruct us to do so. Our mission is to bring him to Tiali as quickly as possible."

"Put yourself in his place. If you were the one Bocar had fetched without any explanation, you would fill your pants. Let's tell him. We can ask him not to repeat our conversation."

"Am I your superior or not? We will do as the prince ordered, may it please God. If you overstep your instructions your head will roll on the ground of Mboupbène."

Tior, clever as a monkey, agile as a hare and quick as a snake, made his way through the trees and fell half-dead from exhaustion at his father's feet.

Mayacine was getting ready to give thanks to God for the third prayer of the day. The kettle, filled with water for the ritual cleansing, emptied over a stunned Tior, who little by little regained his wits. Mayacine, troubled, forgot his ablutions. His back to the East, he prayed to *rakas* whose verses had nothing to do with the Koran.

Then after a quick *salmalekoum,* he took the child by his shoulders and lifted him off the ground, convinced that Tior had been the victim of supernatural spirits. Tior gasped for air.

"Run and hide. Disappear before it's too late, father. Soldiers are arriving from Tiali. They are coming to get you. They will take you away. Those are Bocar's orders. What have you done?"

"Nothing I could be ashamed of, son. I don't have to flee. I have neither lied, stolen, nor killed. I will wait for them.

"Wives, children, brothers, and sisters, all of you, listen to me. I don't know what to expect. I hardly have time for a long speech. Every second counts. Be allies, be united. Respect the sacred bonds of the family, apply the rights of the eldest, such are my last wishes.

"Tior, saddle my horse. Woman, prepare my traveling clothes. Let us wait for the Lord's will."

A short time after Mayacine's instructions to his family, the court messengers arrived. Hardly had the customary greetings been exchanged and the horses rested than Mayacine told them, "It is getting late. Let us take to the road. I must not keep my prince waiting."

The two men looked at each other, impressed with the fortitude shown by their host. Still aching from their hard ride, they had to overcome their fatigue and once more take the road to Tiali.

It was late when the riders reached their destination. The town was steeped in profound silence, interrupted only by the occasional rustling of a leaf or other noises of the night. The moon, high in the starlit sky, guided the travelers who rode single file towards the palace. From the depths of the jungle arose the pervasive, musty odor of dead leaves. Mayacine was praying. His heart heavy, he nervously beat the flanks of his horse.

The palace gates opened and Prince Bocar appeared. The messengers disappeared as if by magic. Mayacine, barely able to stand on his feet after the hard ride, followed the prince with uncertain steps. After a barely audible talk with Bocar behind closed doors and shutters, Mayacine saddled his horse and headed back towards Mboupbène, murmuring incantations all the way.

• • •

Mayacine's unexpected journey had attracted numerous relatives and friends who solicitously kept watch and waited for news of him. The women were lamenting.

The *marabout,* hastily summoned, had ordered the sacrifice of a spotless white lamb and the distribution of bowls of soured milk to the children.

The men of the family recited the Koran. At dawn, overcome by anxiety and fatigue, they fell asleep. Not long after, the lusty crowing of the rooster wakened them. Far away the dull thud of hooves pounding the earth could be heard.

Mayacine and his horse entered the courtyard at the end of their strength. "Nothing serious, my friends, only peace." Those were his only words.

• • •

The next morning Lala was about to leave the hut after giving her husband his customary massage, when he stopped her.

"Thank you, Lala," Mayacine said to her. "As God is my witness, these thanks come from the bottom of my heart. You have always been a model wife and perfect in every way. I have always had faith that fortune would smile on your children.

"Now call Fary. I have to tell you about a matter of the greatest importance."

A few days later Fary left to visit her maternal aunt in the village of Ndouli.

The north wing of the palace in Tiali had been subjected to an onslaught of masons and decorators, all charged with the task of quick yet sumptuous changes to welcome an important guest. All the spacious apartments were provided with immense verandas. Wide openings where the air could circulate added to the coolness of the large rooms.

Woven *pagnes* with different motifs depicting various pastoral hunting and fishing scenes covered the carved wooden furniture.

Bocar's wives, their hands and feet blackened with henna, were trying out new hairdos. Secretly they prepared new wardrobes, determined to outdo all the women of Tiali during the festivities sure to accompany the arrival of such an illustrious guest.

The coach stopped in front of the new buildings. A strange-looking person got out. His weird *boubou* dragged on the ground. An enormous turban covered his head and part of his face. Lifting the tails of his *boubou,* he followed the dwarf who had come to receive him.

He crossed a number of rooms, hallways, and verandas, which formed a true maze to end up in an immense, paneled room, the center of which was occupied by a mattress put on a bamboo bedstand.

Benches made of the same material as the bed filled the corners of the room. On one of them cowered a shadowy figure, her back to the lights shining from a number of small lamps made of cotton wicks burning in grease.

The dwarf had disappeared as if by magic. The shadow moved. It was the procuress of Tiali. She came up to the guest, unwound the turban, and pulled off his *boubou.*

Fary appeared, as breathtakingly beautiful as a fairy from the legends. Her hair was dressed in a multitude of little braids which fell to her neck, adorned with pearls and jewels. Her white blouse and her white *pagne* were the symbols of her purity. She was sublime.

Fary submitted to the ministrations of the beldame like a statue of stone. The old woman was enchanted. This girl had the beauty of the devil, beauty to damn a saint. For the first time since she had assumed her duties in the palace she was in the presence of such brilliance.

"My child," she told Fary, "Now you are the fourth wife of Prince Bocar. For security reasons your marriage must be kept strictly secret for one month. Your own life and that of your family depend on secrecy. Only a small number of people know about it. It has been celebrated here with your parents' consent.

"Your apartments have been laid out in such a way that no one can enter them without the consent of Mayoro, your husband's right-hand man.

"The court is expecting an illustrious guest, Diakher Makoumba Malick, the prince's cousin and a famous warrior from Tatane. He will be here for a few days. He will occupy part of the new apartments. This is a strategy of our sovereign, who counts on distracting the attention of his subjects, especially of the spies who pollute the court."

The only answer the old woman received was an impassive face and sealed lips.

Attributing her silence to shyness and emotion, the old woman continued her counsel with fervor.

"Be patient, sweet, and loving and you can do as you like with Bocar. He has rare intelligence and a will of steel. He never reverses his decisions. The complex his affliction gives him is also his strength. His courage is legendary."

"However, his heart overflows with generosity for those who understand him. Them he loves. Your life here will be what you make of it."

Fary remained silent, but her heart was full of gratitude to this old, gossipy woman who had advised her on her future behavior.

• • •

Bocar arrived soon after the procuress had left, hopping like a monkey from the jungle. A leering smile revealed wild animal teeth and widened his bulging eyes which had flames of desire dancing in them.

Fary looked at Bocar without flinching, but this horror, this weird animal who in a few moments would defile her body, made her ill with disgust.

Her good resolves were going to melt like sugar in water. She looked around the room to find a weapon to smash his enormous head when a voice from her innermost being brought her back to reason.

Perturbed, the prince looked to the ground. He was standing there undecided, like a child who has been caught in some mischief. She obviously intimidated him.

"Your life will be what you make it."

Conscious of the hold she would have over him in the future and aware that all depended on how she acted at this very instant, she blew out the lamps and went to bed.

The feeling of this loathsome body on hers sickened her more than when she had encountered the big ape in the jungle. He slithered over her body like a snake, fondling her breasts, her neck, her arms, hurting her chest with his big head.

Fary tried to muster all the strength and will power she had left in order not to faint. Under the mattress her hands gripped the bed so hard that the wood cut into her fingers and tore her flesh, but nothing eased this intolerable assault. Her legs locked together in a last surge of revolt. Her innermost being could not accept in these ultimate moments what had seemed acceptable before. She fought with all her strength, opposing, categorically refusing him, when suddenly, as if endowed with a mysterious power, he overcame her resistance and made her his.

●　●　●

At dawn she was visited by the old crone who was to minister to her body. After a long massage the old woman bathed her in a large tub filled with essences of plants which miraculously took away all Fary's traces of fatigue.

The bed was made and the room tidied. Fary was offered a bowl of cornmeal mush on which floated golden cream and large globs of butter. Despite the cream and butter, Fary could not swallow the mush.

The prince had disappeared. There was not a trace of him left in the room. Fary asked herself if she were not the victim of hallucinations, so unreal all seemed to her. Never had she felt more alone, more abandoned. The secret arrival of her friend, Coura, in the course of the morning was to change her life considerably.

Alone in the room, Coura undid her bundle. It contained several varieties of plants and they were no ordinary plants. They were Sokhna's wedding gift.

Coura, intimidated by her strange mission, avoided looking at her friend. Now Fary understood why the women of Mboupbène hated Sokhna so much. Sokhna was dangerous!

Once their husbands were caught in her net they could not get free again. Her weapons were these aphrodisiac plants which more than any clean house, good cooking, or fresh laundry ensured her a special place in Bocar's harem.

The queen mother retained the hatred she had conceived at her first meeting with Fary. She would never forgive her for being *griotte,* untouchable, but especially loathed her because she was now the one who received all her son's attentions.

Not a day went by that the queen mother did not surreptitiously enter Fary's apartments with an insult on her lips.

Fary never reacted to her snubs. Charming and polite, she rather tried to win her over. Her long curtsies, her lowered head and her soft, docile voice, all her submissiveness was an effort to overcome the resentment against her.

Aside from the procuress, Fary's only visitor was Mayoro who came to inquire about her needs and brought her the latest news from Mboupbène.

The prince came only late at night. He was in love with her. He adored her. Her feminine intuition did not deceive her. She was sure of his love. She felt it in his furtive caresses, saw it in his moist eyes filled with admiration for her, and sensed it in all the delicate attentions he showed her, albeit awkwardly.

● ● ●

The two horses were grazing side by side in the sparsely covered grass of the hills. Bocar and Mayoro, up since the first crow of the rooster, had had a vigorous early morning ride. They now were resting at the foot of a tree which once more watched over their confidences.

Lying on his back, his hand folded under his neck, Bocar looked up counting the fruit of the baobab tree, veritable stalactites suspended from bare, skinny branches reaching into the still misty sky like a giant skeleton.

"Mayoro," he suddenly said to his *beuk-nek,* "Do you believe in God?"

"Yes, of course, my prince," Mayoro stuttered. "On my father's belt, I believe in Him! Sometimes I forget my prayers and my hands and my tongue occasionally play tricks on me. Sometimes my feet take me where I shouldn't go. That sort of thing happens. To tell the truth, I prefer my ancestors' religion. It offers more freedom than these Muslim practices with their innumerable constraints. That is what I think. On my father's belt, that's what I think!"

"Stop swearing on your father's belt, you infidel. You are not a heathen, but a Muslim. Swear it by God, the Prophet, the Holy Scriptures."

Mayoro could not believe his ears. Incredulously, he stared at Bocar with wide eyes. He didn't dare pronounce the words forming in his throat. As if able to read his thoughts, the prince came to his aid.

"I surprise you, don't I? You thought me a heathen. Well, I was. I had always begrudged the *marabouts'* interfering in our lives, preaching in our pagan country this Muslim religion with its rigorous rules. But I had a dream, a revelation which is at the origin of my new religion."

"Since your revelation or since your wedding night," Mayoro thought to himself. That little Fary wasted no time. Already she had converted him! How far was she going to go? Still dizzy, he wanted to change this thorny subject and asked in an uncertain voice, "Don't you think it would be about time to present Fary to the court of Tiali, my Prince? I try to keep her presence secret, but you never know. The court is full of spies. I implore you, it is an urgent matter."

Faced with Bocar's silence, the *beuk-nek* repeated, "it is an urgent matter."

"I am thinking about it, Mayoro. It is one of my chief concerns. I am certain of my authority, yet I am apprehensive about my people's reaction. Fary is the most precious gift I have received on this earth. I would defend her to the last drop of my blood. To me, she is more important than the crown of Tiali."

"Without which you wouldn't have her in the first place," Mayoro mumbled under his breath.

"I will do everything in my power to make her the happiest woman in the world. I know that she was forced into this marriage. How? I don't know. I would give my life for her happiness. My mother will help me. Up to now her motives remain a mystery to me. First, she chose a *griotte,* an untouchable, a woman of caste, to be my wife. Then she chose Fary, the very one I desired with all my heart. It all defies understanding.

"Mayoro!"

"My prince?"

"Enough of this hesitation. It is decided. The presentation of my wife, Fary Mayacine Mboup, will take place seven days hence at the court of Tiali. I want her to have a unique wardrobe, jewels which will make our women pale with envy. Go into the villages and bring back treasures. I will pay any price.

"Let your *marabout* do everything necessary to protect my wife, let him arm her against the evil she may expect not only from the court, but also from her co-wives. I am counting on you to anticipate all eventualities awaiting her."

Once again, poor Mayoro was confounded by Bocar's unexpected reactions.

Unceasingly, tom-toms drummed out the special beat, seven beats for especially serious situations. The entire population of Tiali was to attend an important assembly. Dignitaries, the heads of families, and the women and children hurried to the amphitheater where the meeting was to take place. Excitement was at its peak.

"You, the people of Tiali, of Ndouli, of Ndom, of Tatane, you the people of Mboupbène and its surrounding counties, you, my friends and relatives, I bid you welcome. This is a gathering of peace. May peace be eternal in our country.

"I am your sovereign. I am also your friend. I have to account to you for my actions, even if they are private, to reinforce the confidence, the affection, the friendship, the respect which unite us. More than once you have proven your attachment to me and I hope it will be the same today."

Murmurs of approbation and cheering resounded in the amphitheater. Bocar moved a bamboo screen which separated his wife from the crowd, seized her hand, which she gave him after a moment's hesitation, and made her step forward.

Fary was draped in beautiful cloth and sparkling with jewels. Bocar led her into the circle of dumbfounded people where some, paralyzed by the spectacle, devoured her with their eyes. Others, stricken by the strange contrast of the couple, almost fainted.

"Here is the reason for this meeting."

A frantic ovation greeted the prince's words.

"I present my fourth wife before God and you, the people. Here is Princess Fary Mboup, daughter of Mayacine and Lala Mboup."

There was deadly silence. Mayacine and his friends advanced and saluted the bewildered assembly by a bow from the waist.

• • •

Later, Fary would give half of her life to relive those wonderful moments when thousands of men, women, and children prostrated themselves at her feet, their faces to the ground. They moved silently like ghosts as if the world had come to an end, as if the earth

had suddenly opened under their feet. Little by little, cries could be heard. Voices clamored for water. Bocar's wives, outrageously painted and dressed in elaborate gowns dripping with gold, fell like flies.

Confusion, surprise, and emotion reigned supreme.

Fary was assaulted by looks. She was cursed. Her most seductive smile, her most disdainful looks, alternately met with disapproving murmurs from all sides the instant Bocar moved away from her.

"How long has she been in the palace?"

"God knows. Perhaps since the sheep came?"

"Ah, that's the girl who accompanied Mayacine. It's not surprising. Insolent and ambitious. You should have seen how cold-bloodedly she looked at the queen mother, with what effrontery, and how her eyes took in the riches of the palace."

"She is too beautiful for a human being. I wonder if she is not a spirit who took the shape of a woman."

"She will make a nice pair with her monkey. It seems she is supposed to be the reincarnation of the protecting spirit of Tiali."

"Birds of a feather flock together."

Bocar's arrival silenced the voices. His presence made her immune to their taunts. He was her shield against the poisoned arrows assailing her from all directions.

Surrounded by slaves fanning her, covered with a train sweeping the ground, and accompanied by the dull throbs of the tom-toms, Fary entered the apartments now officially designated for her.

For eight days Tiali celebrated Fary's wedding to Bocar. The people, some liking it, some not, put on a good face and took part in the festivities: tom-toms, wrestling matches, horse racing, chants and dances. From morning to night slaves put at her disposal fanned Fary, massaged her body, prepared her food, her linens, and kept her house tidy. The chords of the *khalam* were strummed all day long. Young *griots,* as her ancestor Sakhor once had done, sat at her feet singing her family history or that of the prince.

She discovered she had glorious ancestors of unheard-of prowess. The laurel leaves of glory now seemed to abound in her family. Her ancestors, once inveterate pagans, getting drunk on palm wine and snuffing tobacco, were suddenly transformed into veritable saints, into *walious,* symbols of purity and abstinence.

● ● ●

"Keep your eyes and ears open, my child. Be very careful. Many people will try to be close to you to satisfy their ambition. They underestimate your youth. Think before you speak. Discuss things with your husband. You will always find an attentive ear and advice you need at my side."

Those were the words spoken to her now by the queen mother. She remained a big enigma in Tiali. Her presence at Fary's side when she was presented to the court, her haughty air defying the assembly, her hand on Fary's shoulder, all proved she had accepted her.

• • •

The marriage of the prince of Tiali was also celebrated in the villages subject to the principality. In Mboupbène the festivities brought many differences of opinion. The young people made up a lot of songs of which the most popular was:

Woman, clear your field, labor and plant,
to your children tomorrow the harvest belongs.
Lala Mboup in the field of Mayacine
has managed to pull out the nettle's roots.
Patience, modesty, and wisdom
made Fary princess of Tiali.
Woman, clear your field, labor and plant,
to your children tomorrow the harvest belongs.

• • •

Some families in Mboupbène could not forgive Mayacine for having kept the marriage a secret. They had showed solicitude and friendship when he had to go on his sudden journey to Tiali. They felt that their compassion had been rewarded with distrust and injury.

Others were jealous because Fary and not their own daughters had been chosen. They did not cease to speak ill of Fary's conduct and her father's opportunism. They created a terrible reputation for Fary. Suddenly she had become shameless, pretentious, and ambitious, a gold-digger who stopped at nothing to reach her goal.

She must have used her already tarnished charms to corrupt poor Bocar, who could not see farther than his nose, and was content with leftovers.

Their hatred went so far as to forbid the young to sing the

songs about Fary in their family circles. They beat their innocent children without mercy if they dared hum the cursed verses.

• • •

In Tiali a similar thunderstorm was brewing. On this particular day a secret meeting was held in the principality at the house of Tiob Ndiaye, Bocar's cousin and member of his cabinet.

The assembly included a good number of people, dissatisfied dignitaries who cooked up intrigues or were in league against the regime. Bocar's marriage, an imponderable element, was questioned, but actually it had little to do with their personal griefs and political ambitions.

The members of the assembly were getting angry and noisy. The racket attracted Mayoro who, fleeing the moonlight had wandered into the bushes to find a suitable spot to relieve his bladder. His ears perked up as he listened. He could hear different voices.

"Bestir yourselves, my friends, it is time to act. What are we? Human beings, normal ones, commanded by a monster, a nothing, a dwarf, who leads us by the nose like children, who always makes us do his bidding. A *griotte* in his bed? A calamity! An infamy! Soon disaster will befall us. She will stay here. She will bring her children here and her dead will be buried here."

"Ah, never, and we mean never! The *griots* have their own graveyard. It is at Mboupbène. The rule is for everybody. There are no exceptions. Bocar himself has ordered it this way and it's up to him to see that his orders are carried out."

"He is capable of revoking them when the time comes."

"He will never accept it. He has filled his cup. Let him drink it down to the bitter dregs."

"Who does he think he is? He marries a *griotte* and tells us about it after the deed is done. Today it is a marriage, tomorrow the State."

"And did you see our dear *griots?* They have become bold, proclaiming equality. Soon they will rob us of our privileges, our fortunes, our women."

"Let's make an end of it. Let the traitor perish."

"How?"

"By knife."

"Where?"

"In the mosque during Friday's services. It will be difficult to blame the crime on anyone in particular in the confusion of a big crowd."

"Since when does Bocar go to the mosque? I'm really learning some new ones today."

"Since his wedding. It seems that is one of his *griotte's* accomplishments. Not only did he convert to this Muslim religion, but his whole family with him. I heard it said that he plans to enlarge the building and will issue a decree to convert all his subjects to his new religion. We will be the first ones."

"I can hardly believe you. Bocar in a mosque? Is this the floods? The end of the world? And what is he going to do about his daily ration of mead and *rikless*?

"It seems he no longer touches alcohol. That's another change the untouchable has wrought."

"Let us agree on one last point before we separate."

They did not have the time. In a flash they were surrounded by Bocar's guards whom Mayoro had summoned. The traitors were taken away to await their punishment.

Falla and her co-wife Yande were talking on their way to the market. "Let me ask you once more, Falla. Have you looked in the mirror lately? You look like a fried herring. You are as scrawny as a juniper tree before rainy season. You will surely die if you go on like this. Think of your children. Bocar won't mourn your loss. He has better things to do.

"I take the liberty of speaking to you like this because I consider you a sister who nursed at the same breast and who alone would dare call attention to our bad breath. To let yourself die because of a marriage with a *griotte*! A *griotte* who is paid to sing your praise.

"No, Falla, no. You don't eat properly, you don't dress well anymore, and you cry for no reason at all. The evil tongues are wagging behind your back. You can't blame Bocar for neglecting you. You look worse than Nogaye, the beggar woman.

"I would advise you to accept your misfortune with patience and to follow my example. You have seen me, Yande Madaga Nidaye. A woman like myself won't make me lose my head. Unless she was something other than a woman, which I doubt.

"However, there is one thing that puzzles me. Have you watched the queen mother? I am certain she had something to do with this marriage. She did not disapprove of this union which would have killed her only a short while ago. She accepted it with disconcerting *ease*. This situation does not make sense at all. Mayoro, too, has become as invisible as the wind. It's a plot, I am sure of it.

"I heard about a *marabout* in Ndiom. Since Bocar's new love leaves us all the free time we want, we will go to see him after the harvest. I have had my trouble with Deguène, the first one. However, I am still here. I won't give them the satisfaction of gloating over my suffering, neither her nor the dwarf."

Falla spoke at last.

"The dwarf also belongs to us. You are undoubtedly right, but believe me, I am not suffering from the frustration of defending my position. I am reacting because of disgust and disdain. To have a dwarf for a husband, all right, but a *griotte* for a co-wife is too much. She is a wife with the same rights as we have, if not more.

"I am ashamed for my children who later on will have *griots* for half-brothers. This blemish on our family is what breaks my heart."

Deguène, Bocar's number one wife, full of pride, was reserve itself. Her place as first wife imposed a certain attitude on her, a noble conduct, and forbade her any rebellion which would have lowered her prestige at the court of Tiali.

Falla and Yande were co-wives with whom she kept up a courteous relationship. For her, Fary would always be a *griotte*, a woman of caste, and nothing more.

Her older daughters, who were about the same age as Fary, were full of resentment. They saw a rival in her and the source of future misfortune. Already some of their friends had changed camps. Their *griots*, ambitious for a more brilliant career, no longer sang their praises but abandoned them for Fary, the intruder.

On that particular morning a messenger arrived at Mayacine's house and knocked at the door. "They are waiting for you," he told Mayacine.

The dignitaries of Mboupbène had called a meeting at the Imam's house. As soon as Mayacine arrived the debates began. The Imam was the first to speak.

"We are gathered here today to discuss a matter which concerns all of us, the *griots* of Mboupbène, represented here by every one of you. It is time to act like men, to get up our courage and face the enemy. We are not asking him for alms, we are asking only for our rights, these rights legally ours but which have been taken from us, falsified by a society thirsting for domination.

"We have always been considered slaves, men without importance, censured for no good reason. Excluded from the society of Tiali, we are rejected along with our laws, our customs. We have had enough of this segregation, of this so-called separatist ideology.

"We want to participate actively in the government, vote and have a right to speak. Yes, I am saying a right to speak. We no longer want to be considered outcasts with evil blemishes or like exiles only good enough to be sacrificed in battle.

"We are asking neither for charity nor mercy. We ask for what is due us—rehabilitation."

All approved, nodding their heads. Mody succeeded the Imam.

"The Imam is right. His words express the feelings of each one of us present. So there is nothing to be added. I would simply say that we are counting on you, Mayacine. Your daughter is the prince's wife. That gives you some rights. Given your privileged position as father-in-law, it won't be difficult for you to speak to him and to submit our requests to him, to convince him.

"He is the supreme ruler of Tiali. All the decisions come from him. To begin with, the most urgent matter is the right to vote, the right to be represented in his government."

• • •

Mayacine was perplexed. His daughter's marriage had made him the most sought-after person in Mboupbène. Ever since his daughter's wedding he had been constantly asked to convey grievances to the prince of Tiali, but he had hardly expected an errand of such dimensions.

• • •

It was late when he knocked at his daughter's door. "Once again, daughter, I am counting on you to obtain your husband's consent to the requests I am forced to submit to him. My honor is at stake. Many of those asking for these rights have no motivation. They are guided only by jealousy and meanness. They want to tarnish my reputation. They want to see me cornered, put to the test, expecting each time to see me defeated.

"A toothpick in their mouth, they polish their teeth to laugh at my downfall. Thank God it has never happened that way until now. God does not grant us the death of our enemy. Though I am ashamed to ask you once more to intercede with your husband, I have no other recourse. He has made so many concessions to me that I dare no longer ask him to his face."

Fary promised to intercede.

A wonderful aroma of peanuts wafted from the kitchen and tickled Fary's nostrils. She went to join Coura, a wonderful cook, who every night prepared delicious meals with which to regale the prince.

Fary was learning to cook from her friend. Coura was most discreet. Being very circumspect, she appeared only at the very instant Fary needed her. Between the two women there existed a true telepathic friendship. Coura was the friend, the counsellor, the governess. Since she had arrived, Fary had with difficulty gotten rid of the old procuress.

When Fary told Coura about Mayacine's request, a smile twinkled in Coura's eyes. She did not possesss that dazzling beauty which attracts men like honey does flies, but her well-proportioned little figure, her shining teeth, and full lips made her one of Mboupbène's favorites. Her sudden naughtiness could make even Sokhna blush. At present it was Fary who lowered her eyes in front of Coura.

"Your father is lucky. Bocar is going to have his favorite dish tonight: *bassi,* a cous-cous which I took special pains with. It is to tip the scales in your favor."

She bent over her pot and lifted the lid. Pieces of yam, squash, meat, and beans mingled, bubbling in a sauce of creamy peanut paste. The pot with its delicious contents and ambrosial aroma assailed Fary's nostrils and made her mouth water. Coura reached for a calabash and shook the cous-cous which smelled excitingly of *diwou-nior.*

"Yes, luck will be on your side. I will season my sauce a little more with Sokhna's herbs. That is nothing to sneeze at. Make yourself beautiful, intoxicate him with incense, perfume, and sweet words. Once again you will get your way."

"I expect to get my way if your plants don't kill him first."

Not long after her father's visit Fary started having dizzy spells and terrible fits of vomiting. Coura, worried, diagnosed her trouble as malaria. She started treating her with different brews and made her mush which the patient retched up after the first spoonful.

Coura was watching Fary closely. Her inquisitive gaze was constantly on her friend observing her from head to toe, looking at her belly, her swollen breasts. She decided to question her: "Fary, how long has it been since you menstruated?"

Fary did not answer.

"I don't have my grandmother's knowledge, but your swollen breasts, your dizzy spells, your nausea, your headaches, are all signs of pregnancy even though your belly is flat. You don't have to be a sorcerer to know it. Those are the signs of a malaria crisis my mother always claims to suffer from only to present us with a brother or sister soon after."

Fary still did not utter one word.

"Instead of playing the mute, you had better answer me so that I can take the necessary steps to protect you and the child."

Fary hardly recognized her friend. Tiali had changed the docile Coura into a self-assured, outspoken woman. She had taken on Fary's role. In Mboupbène it had been Fary who was the leader and always had the last word. At present she had become the little girl who knew nothing and was constantly being lectured by a new, amazing Coura.

Her desperate look full of fear and her silent tears softened her guardian. Coura gently lifted Fary's head, held the calabash to her lips, and made her swallow a few sips of soup.

"Yes, I am expecting a child. What would be another woman's greatest happiness is a tragedy for me. I live in fear and apprehension. I cannot get the question out of my mind. Will the child look like his father?"

"Did you not know what risks you were taking when you married Bocar? You made your choice. Now you will have to accept the consequences. Does he know about your condition?"

"Not yet."

"He soon will. His intuition will help him."

"I hate him in spite of his love and his attentions."

"You hate him, yet you share his bed." Coura smiled strangely.

"Why are you smiling?"

"It's the surprise, the mystery, the way you have changed. Providence decides our destiny. I was convinced that you would be a princess after Sokhna predicted it, for I have blind faith in her. But that you would marry a dwarf is a possibility I would never have believed. Knowing you, I would have said 'no' with conviction. I would have said 'no' even with a knife at my throat. And yet, it happened.

"What has that marriage brought you? A title, the life of a princess, a few changes in the law in favor of the *griots*. For all that, we are still outcasts, untouchables.

"*Gouye Gueol,* our cemetery, bears witness to this shameful segregation. What were you trying to destroy? Injustice? That you will never do. To sacrifice your youth to a dwarf who loves you, certainly, but who remains a monster nevertheless.

"You can fool others, but never me. You don't love him. He disgusts you. I often can see murder in your eyes and I pray to God every minute to prevent disaster. You would be capable of killing Bocar, Fary."

"Why such vehemence, such lecturing? You have not stopped berating me since you came here. Do you think I am unfeeling? I suffer from this life more than you could ever imagine.

"Yes, I would be capable of killing Bocar. I hate him. It is not lack of desire to strangle him or smash his enormous head that has kept me from doing it. Little do you know me. I can overcome my instincts no matter what they are when I once set myself a goal. This one I will attain if it is at the cost of my own life."

"When I see how obstinate you are, I ask myself which of us is right. But why do you so stubbornly pursue a goal which is impossible to attain?"

"The word impossible does not belong here. I shall reach this goal to fight for equal rights for all men and to erase every trace of humiliation our race has suffered. I swear it on all that is sacred to me in this world and in the next."

"Now my lady is raving. I have never seen such a stubborn woman. You are used to getting your way, but this time it is a dead-end street."

After this discussion Coura did not bring up the subject again. All through Fary's pregnancy she looked after her friend with tenderness and solicitude.

Fary gave birth to a boy. The prince was ecstatic. The birth of a son had transformed him. He smiled constantly, baring his goat's teeth, hopping about on his short legs like a grasshopper in a millet field. His son was his own portrait. Preoccupied with his own happiness, he never noticed his wife's silence, her gauntness, and her indifference to the child.

● ● ●

Coura, who had come to bring millet mush to her friend, stopped transfixed at the threshold. Fary's face had become a terrifying, murderous mask. It was bathed in perspiration, her nostrils flaring, her lower lip bitten and bleeding. Her breath came like a whistle. Her eyes looked daggers at the child. Her right hand, fingers spread out and curved in like the claws of a vulture, slowly advanced towards the child. Her left hand was on her breast. Coura's yell stopped the hand that fell on the fragile wrinkled neck, so disproportionate to the enormous head of the innocent child who slept, his little fists closed like any baby in the world.

Fary fell on the bed and shed all the tears within her, convinced that she was the unhappiest woman in the world. After experiencing all the difficult problems of pregnancy, the apprehension, the fear of the delivery, the feeling within her being and fibres of her flesh of the baby's kicking, his furtive movements, the observing of the miraculous changes in her body, the inexplicable love, and the unequalled pride of an expectant woman, to have gone through all this only to give birth to a monster.

"No, no," she sobbed. "I don't want a monster. I will kill him. You stopped me today, but you won't the next time. Do you remember Gana, Coura? You told me: 'Marry him. Your children will be as beautiful as angels.'"

Coura picked up the child and held him to her breast. Her face was contorted with rage. Her expression, usually so friendly, had become as stern as a mask.

"You are at the end of your rope, did I not warn you? Your regrets are too late and they are quite useless. You married a dwarf. You should expect your children to be dwarves.

"Forget Gana. He belongs to the past. 'I know how to overcome my instinct when I have set myself a goal,'" she mimicked Fary. "My lady thought she was strong enough to overcome such snags, but she flounders at the first obstacle that comes along. This is only the beginning. What is going to happen to you on the way to your famous goal? You will need breathing spells, strength, courage, and lucidity to face the numerous traps laid for you which you don't even see in the blindness of your incredible ambitions.

"Swallow your murderous instincts. This child is not responsible for anything. He did not ask to be born. From today on I will watch over him. His life will be spent between the nurse and me. If not, we shall be the disgrace of Mboupbène."

Tiali was seething with excitement. New buildings were to be added to the palace. The prince himself was overseeing the work, harassing the workmen, who, intrigued by the sudden interest, were mocking him.

"This is the third time he has had me do the roof over; the

straw is never properly tied together."

"Don't complain," said another, "I am at my fifth frame. He never finds them strong enough, as if it were the first time I had ever done this work."

Malick, bucket in hand, joined the conversation.

"What bit the prince? Since when is he interested in construction, particularly in masonry? I can't seem to get a proper mixture. He makes me add water every time. I've got it just right. Let's hope the wind which blew him out here this morning will take him back to his palace tonight."

"Not a chance," answered Aliou.

"And why not?" Samba asked.

"The fat is in the fire at the palace."

All the workmen left their trowels, saws and ladders to gather around Aliou, who was the most listened-to informer because his fiancée was a loyal member of the prince's staff.

Aliou was still holding the stalk of bamboo he had been cutting to make beds and benches. Full of self-importance, he beamed.

"There has been a violent quarrel between Deguène and the queen mother," said he, confident of the importance of this news.

"That's nothing new," a voice said deprecatingly.

"You are wrong. This time it is really something. Princess Deguène, the first of the name, has openly insulted the queen mother. She reproached her in front of a choice audience for putting a *griotte,* an untouchable, in her son's bed. At this, the old woman had the vapors.

"Tiali was rejoicing when my lady recovered her wits, brought round by flasks and powders and incense, and told her daughter-in-law, 'Fary Mboup is the princess of Tiali. She is young, beautiful and distinguished. Her son will be the heir to the throne!' Whereupon Deguène fainted."

"That's against the law," Deguène's cousin replied. Blood was speaking. He was defending his relatives. "According to the law, the eldest son is the heir.

"It's my nephew who must be prince of Tiali. I'll talk to the dignitaries."

They all laughed at the prospect of such an incongruous undertaking.

"By the way, what does he look like, this new-born babe?" Ali inquired.

"The spitting image of his father," a voice murmured. As the falsetto voice of the prince approached, the laborers dispersed.

The baptism became the source of new festivities. The people of Mboupbène were the guests of honor. Fary's parents had started to prepare for the great event as soon as they got wind of their daughter's first attack of nausea.

Disregarding the tradition which says that projects preceeding the birth attract bad luck, the *griots* had gone all out to make clothes, jewels, hairdos, and shoes. They wanted to make this baptism more sumptuous than any in Tiali's history. Sheep were sacrificed. Pieces of meat fried in animal fat accumulated in vast barrels which, together with barrels of oil, cous-cous, corn, fried cakes, an impressive quantity of *pagnes,* cloth, and *boubous* made their way to Tiali, piled on horse-drawn wagons to the sound of the tom-toms.

Mboupbène wanted to impress Tiali, the seat of power. Thanks to Bocar's generosity, the village had become rich and important with flourishing trade.

• • •

Fary's throne dominated the important assembly which united the whole population of Tiali and its territories.

The princess's large *boubou,* completely embroidered by the seamstresses of Mboupbène, swept the ground. Her numerous braids were adorned with pearls of amber, silver, and gold. Gold glittered at her neck, at her wrists, and at her ankles.

The cloth dyers of Mboupbène had worked miracles. Each hamlet was represented at the festivities by a dozen women all dressed alike in a light blue *boubou* coming to the knees, dark blue *pagnes,* their hair dressed in small braids coming down to the neck and their hands and feet blackened with henna. Sets of rings adorned their hands. The tattooed lips and gums made their teeth seem even brighter.

The men, a dozen from each hamlet, wore white starched *boubous* over billowing pants. Red bonnets covered their heads.

Prince Bocar, seated at Fary's side, disappeared under a flowing, beautifully embroidered coat. His throne attracted all eyes. It was an enormous armchair, hung with white silk on which sparkled a golden sun which circled the dwarf's enormous head like a crown.

Mayacine had the place of honor at the prince's right. The three *boubous* he wore on top of each other restricted his movements. The *palmane*, a dark blue *boubou*, was more than half a century

old. It had belonged to his ancestor Sakhor Mboup, and since his death had gone to the eldest male descendant.

The vassal of Ndouli, Cheik Sidi Baba, whose ancestors descended from the Moors, could be recognized by his long bronze pipe circled in silver and his enormous black turban wound around his head in the style of the Touaregs. At his side he had a handful of his men moving about as silently as ghosts.

The vassal of Tatane, Massamba Maye, the biggest hunter of the region, was the attraction of the day. His right hand, adorned with claws, rested on a cane with a silver pommel. Lion and panther fangs embellished his *boubou* and graced his wrists and neck. A bonnet made of a ram's skin adorned with two horns covered his head. He was approached by all with great deference.

The famous horseman, Mafatim Maye, who had won the grand prize in the Tiali equestrian show, represented the territory of Ndam. The trophies of his victories, multicolored frills and ribbons, adorned his chest.

Ndiom, famous for the influence of its wise men and its *marabouts,* was represented by the venerable Tyero Alpha, head of the spiritual family of the area. His long serene face with its majestic beard smiled at the people respectfully approaching him.

He was dressed in white from his *boubou* to his slippers. His right hand rested on an umbrella which served him as a cane. A group of believers surrounded him. One of them at his right kept fanning him. From time to time people prostrated themselves at his feet and kissed his hands.

● ● ●

The people of Tiali avoided the *griots* as if any contact with them would be harmful. The latter felt very much at ease despite these conventional surroundings. They were singing and tossing impertinent remarks back and forth which mortified and dumbfounded the nobles. Mayoro and Coura, at home now in Tiali, talked to their guests.

"Who is this woman whose behind is as flat as a board?

"That's Falla, the second wife. A woman without flesh does not arouse her man. Her bones stick out like thorns. They must often jab the prince."

"And the other one with her scornful mouth, with breasts as big as udders?"

"Yande, a real gossip. She has the tongue of a viper and

spends all her money at the *marabout's*. She would sell her mother for a *gris-gris*."

"Hardly serious. Hands can undo what hands have created."

"And the grandmother who totters from old age, even though she kills herself trying to hold herself straight, her origins must go back farther than millet."

"The first wife, Deguène. She is the uncontested rival of the queen mother, with whom she just had the battle of the century. I am surprised she came. Bocar must have used his heavy guns to bring her to humiliate herself in this way. Deguène's son should really be the heir to the throne."

"Bocar only does what we tell him to. Let's move on."

"You heard 'granny' speak. What eloquence, what lyricism, just to say 'hello'. Really, Tiali is beginning to acquire a sense for good form. Our close contact can't help but give them some polish at last."

"What about the two dimwits? The one with the crooked nose, the other a spitting image of Bocar, as gracious as an elephant."

"The crown princesses! Bocar's eldest daughters. They are to be reckoned with, more dangerous than 'granny', their mother. They have a lot of influence over the prince."

"That one sitting to Fary's left intrigues me. The old one staggering under her jewels and all her *pagnes* one over the other like onion skins?"

"The queen mother. You cannot easily recognize her under her heavy layers of make-up. Vain and impossible. The first lady and also the first gentleman of Tiali, even when her husband was alive, and still today. She was always the one who wore the pants. I wonder what has brought her to our side. Unthinkable! At present, she only lives for Fary."

"That is destiny's revenge. We will make her see stars in plain daylight. We will make her as miserable as she made her husband. An eye for an eye, a tooth for a tooth."

"And the old boy to the prince's right with his bonnet on crooked and his teeth as far apart as furrows?"

"The prince's uncle, the queen mother's brother. He can't stop looking at Sokhna. Underneath his honorable appearance he is the biggest lecher in the court. Pretty buttocks make him lose his head and make a hole in Tiali's finances. Unfortunately, he is in charge of the treasury."

"The young man near the window, he looks suspect to me.

With his powdered face and his painted eyelashes I would rather think he is among the pederasts of whom I have noted a goodly number since our arrival here."

"You are not mistaken. He is one of them. He is the president of the Fairies, a private club. It seems that Bocar is a member. At least, that's what his enemies say. I myself am convinced of the opposite. He has given proof of his manhood many times, the most recent being today's baptism. He is a real man."

"What slander. They couldn't be nastier with us."

"The sister of the Fairies' president likes to say that her mother's milk fell on her brother's sex when she nursed him as a baby. What a tale!"

"Fary had better diaper her son properly. We want a real man."

"I'll see to that. The festivities are about to begin. Let's listen."

• • •

Fary had not lost a word of this conversation. Strange words exchanged by ironic voices, biting and derisive. Several times she had to smile at their impertinence, this spirit so characteristic of her people.

Bintou Malick, one of the prince's numerous cousins, was her first *ndieuke,* her appointed sister-in-law towards whom Fary had specific obligations. They included visits, gifts like a leg of lamb, *tabaski,* the sacrifice of Abraham commemorated each year by the Muslim community.

Bintou began to speak:

"Greetings, relatives from Tiali and Mboupbène. Greetings. I bid you welcome on our soil. As oldest daughter of Bocar's uncle, I speak in the name of the paternal branch which is present here. Our ceremonies are about to begin. For those of you who do not know, the child will carry the name of his valorous paternal grandfather, prince Biram Malick Djiwan.

"We want to thank your daughter here in front of you. She has not tried to separate us. On the contrary, she came, needle in hand, to mend what had been split apart. May God give her in this house a second Biram Malick with all the qualities and the bravery of the first one. I speak sincerely. My words come straight from the heart. Being Bocar's cousin by blood, God will hear my prayers."

• • •

What falsehood. What tendentious compliments! Fary was skeptical of her in-law's sincerity. A look at Assia, who had hoped her daughter would be Bocar's fourth wife, convinced her. No look could be more hostile. Her sister-in-law talked on. Her speech was punctuated by meaningful looks at the group among whom were Deguène and her co-wives, condemning them to disgrace.

"May the Lord grant us to begin with *bissimilahi* and to end with *rahmani rahimi,* the famous preliminaries of the Koran. Let us count the *pagnes.*

"One, two, three . . . . fifty pagnes
One, two, three . . . . . fifty boubous
Two gold bars
Two horns filled with silver nuggets
Two bulls
Twelve rams
Twelve male goats
Two dozen chicken and roosters.

"All of this is given to Fary and her child by the sisters-in-law of the paternal branch."

Fary's maternal side of the family, represented by Lala's niece, began to speak.

"We thank Bocar's family, his friends, his subjects. We especially thank Bocar, for had he made Fary's life difficult, had he neglected her, she would not have had the heart or the means to treat you properly, as you deserve.

"Fary's qualities do not surprise us, her aunts, for she comes by them honestly. Her mother, Lala, who is present here, is an exemplary woman. She could live in a hole with a snake. She is not only Mayacine's wife, but she represents her father, her mother, and us, her sisters, at each family gathering. May God give her in our house another Sakhor Mboup.

"We thank you for your reception. The gifts do you honor, but to prove to you that 'two five-franc pieces are similar,' we double the dowry of Tiali and give it to Fary's sisters-in-law and to their children. And in addition, we give you five sheep, three bowls of cous-cous, five bowls of ginger, and fifty francs for your meals, your drinks and travel expenses. Call your slaves, we will hand them our gifts."

● ● ●

Tiali, the reigning power, had not spoken its last word. Mortified, it replied via Aley, who had leaned close to the queen mother for an instant. "We double the gifts of Mboupbène. We offer them to thank you for having come so far to celebrate this big event with us. This is our last word."

Fary listened impassively to the contest between the two parties. She had faith in her village. She was convinced that it would have the last word.

The assembly had begun to disperse when her friend Sokhna's voice was heard, musical and captivating: "Fary Mayacine Mboup is our daughter, our sister, our friend. Our customs demand that on the baptism of her first child all of her relatives united bestow gifts on her sisters-in-law and their children. This part here," she said pointing to a large pile of cloth, *boubous,* and *pagnes*, "belongs to her mother-in-law, the uncles- and aunts-in-law."

"This lot," she said pointing to another heap of cloth, "is for her sisters-in-law and their children." Without allowing time for a reply, she summoned the drummers and created confusion. "Go ahead, drums, beat me the rhythm."

She threw herself into the circle formed by the *griots,* singing at the top of their voices and clapping their hands as hard as they could. Sokhna's beauty, her charm and elegance held the audience spellbound. She danced gracefully showing her beautiful legs gartered with scarlet *gris-gris.* She danced and sang,

> "We double, we triple,
> We give four times as much.
> Five times as much.
> For a day like today
> is worthy of such.
> Full is our hand
> and even fire can't
> destroy our riches."

Coura also went into the circle, followed by the aunts, the sisters, the girlfriends of the entire community of Mboupbène. Men, women, and children swayed their hips, jumped, sweated, and threw themselves into contortions as if possessed by the devil.

The strident voice of the queen mother tried to pierce this indescribable stampede. She yelled, shouted, asked for silence to double a second time the offering of Mboupbène to prove the inferiority of her vassal. Sokhna, determined to have the last word, went from group to group clapping her hands, shouting, urging on the dancers who, overexcited, were close to madness. The frantic applause of Tiali's inhabitants saluted the beautiful Sokhna.

A short time after the baptism, the prince started to form his new cabinet. The members of the cabinet changed every year following a secret vote in which the dignitaries of Tiali took part. The prince, however, had the final word and could impose a candidate of his own choice on his subjects. Up to now he had always refrained from doing so.

Little by little the audience chamber began to fill up. The men were dressed in their ceremonial robes befitting this special day of the year.

Great was the consternation of the dignitaries when they noted the presence of Mayacine and three other *griots.* Contrary to their usual task of guarding the doors or watching over the princes, they were sitting down ostentatiously, dressed in stately robes worthy of princes of royal blood. The *garnis,* the nobles, mortified by this new state of affairs, conversed with each other, ignoring the newcomers.

Three beats of the drum announced the arrival of the sovereign. The assembly greeted him. He sat down on his throne, his face expressionless. Boma, the man in charge of arms, asked to speak.

"Have the hall cleared, Prince Bocar Djiwan Malick. There are intruders, undesirables among us. We, the *garnis* of Tiali, refuse to sit with those who are not of our race. Those who chant our glory, make our shoes, or forge our spears have no right to be here. No more *masla,* no more pussyfooting.

"Who do you think you are? You impose on us all sorts of novelties; your marriage, then your *griot* son as heir to the throne, and now you welcome untouchables in the assembly hall.

"You make a mockery of the rules established by our ancestors and you walk all over our rights. Leave things as they were. You have no right to profane the heritage of our ancestors."

Bocar stood up on his throne to tower over the audience, giving his high-pitched voice all the authority he could muster. His bulging eyes seemed to come out of his head. He was so furious that his limbs jerked in spasms, beating a rhythm as if he had palsy.

"From now on they are of your race, Boma Malick, since I, your prince, your chief, and supreme commander of Tiali have so decided. These people," he said pointing at Mayacine and his friends, "have the same rights as all of you assembled here from now on. They will vote and they will have their candidate in my cabinet. Nobody can change my plan except over my dead body."

The proud Boma Malick, determined to silence the prince of Tiali, pulled his sword and advanced on him. Bocar flew at him like an eagle and drove his dagger into his enemy's chest. Boma fell to the floor. The session was adjourned.

When the second assembly took place, the *griots* had two representatives in the cabinet.

The people became superstitious. Every time someone attacked the prince of Tiali, misfortune struck. Powerful spirits undeniably protected him. He must really be a genie himself. Henceforth, they no longer contradicted him, but accepted against their will the concessions he granted more and more freely to the *griots*.

A few months after her confinement, Fary went to present her son to Mboupbène. She was accompanied by Mayoro, Coura, some bodyguards, and a princely escort consisting of slaves, livestock, and presents. The ancestors who by tradition and family heritage took care of the child, bathed him in various yellow waters, rubbed him with ointments, made him swallow different concoctions and, by way of scarification, administered medications. Fary was to receive the same treatment.

Thus, the spirit of her ancestors ensured their protection against the evil eye and their immunity to bad intentions.

Fary was happy to be once again on the soil where she had spent her childhood. Mboupbène seemed all new to her. Large compounds and new houses replaced the shacks from previous times. Rich and colorful clothing, the striking exuberance of the population, the amount of foodstuffs and their variety, and the affluence of the market all reflected the opulence and the improved living conditions of the population.

Back from the fields, the men gathered in the shade of the mango tree for their favorite game, the *yote,* a game like checkers.

There before her were all the familiar sights of her childhood, the same backs bent excitedly over the little wooden sticks shooting out from calloused hands. The hands crossed over each other, mingled, or were on top of one another like a devilish dance.

Fary could hardly stop her hands from trembling and inhaled with joy the familiar breeze so characteristic of Mboupbène. She was happy. What joy to have recovered these familiar sights she had missed so much in Tiali!

• • •

With Sokhna she had a regular orgy of fortune telling. "For the moment be content with little," Sokhna told her. "Don't ask for jewels or money. Each thing in its own time. Strengthen your position first of all. You have to fight against three women. Whether you know it or not, they want to harm you and your son. He is the usurper they have to eliminate. Your mother-in-law also must be reckoned with. That is the most important task.

"For the moment providence is on our side. It's in the bag, but we must keep the bag well-tied. Keep Bocar close to you. He must see only you, swear only by you. For him have good meals, soft words, pretty clothes, and tender caresses in bed." Fary lowered her eyes modestly. Sokhna, not at all shy, continued her erotic advice, "Be seductive. Don't hesitate to be a little wild in order to arouse your man. Be a mistress as well as a wife. I have a few artifices in my possession which I will tell you about. You are young and you are beautiful. Make the most of your body. It's your biggest asset. My friends have received some new potions from faraway counties. I'll give you some.

"You have Bocar firmly in your hand. He will be like putty and you can do whatever you like with him. It will be easy for you, for he has had you under his skin for a long time."

• • •

Fary's stay in Mboupbène would have been completely happy had it not been for the hatred she saw in the eyes always looking at her. Each time she appeared she was greeted with insults. Fary did not use her new prestige to have people come and call on her at home. As a daughter of Mboupbène, she wanted to call on her relatives according to tradition, going from door to door. Coura accompanied her friend on all her outings.

"She is the chambermaid and drudge of all work," said Aby, one of her childhood friends. "She leaves her family to go and be a servant to a woman of her own age and rank."

"Correction," Coumba, Gana's wife whose cursed rival Fary had been, added dryly. "Not a woman of her rank, but a princess, even though the princess of a dwarf. I vastly prefer my own life as a *griotte* and Gana's wife. Our son is not a dwarf."

Tears stung Fary's eyes. Coura was just as mortified, but she answered to the ridicule in her own fashion. She burst out laughing at every turn, wiggled her behind in an exaggerated manner and her whole attitude was provocation and defiance. As they went along the river, a hardly audible mumbling answered their greetings. High-pitched voices resounded for a long time afterward.

"What a disgrace! Following Fary like a shadow. She ought to carry her piggyback."

"Did you see her wiggle her behind? She is lost, that one. Her poor parents, they no longer have a daughter."

"And the princess! Did you see her? Madam's feet barely touched the ground. Her dwarf should put wings on her."

"She would surely fly. Her present situation is better than ours, poor mortals that we are whose feet will always touch the ground of Tiali."

"Did you hear, Fary?"

"Yes, Coura. My ears are full of their words."

"Not yet, Fary, that is only the appetizer. The main course and the dessert are yet to come. When I think that it is for these people you have sacrificed your youth and your true love. What a reward! They will never understand your so-called ideals. For them you will always be the intruder, the ambitious climber."

• • •

They saw Gana, hoe in hand, coming back from the fields. Fary's heart beat as if it would burst. She walked towards him with an enchanted smile when he suddenly turned his back and walked away in the opposite direction. Fary could not keep from crying. Coura scolded her, furious.

"Enough, Fary. Not one more tear or I'll leave you right here and now."

Fary could not really understand this jealousy whose extent she realized only now. Even her family was isolated. Her home, once filled with people and noise, was as quiet and deserted as a cemetery.

Her parents were shunned.

She had sacrificed her youth, her life, to defend her people, to fight injustice, the same injustice whose victim she was becoming. But the reaction of an ignorant minority was not going to stand in the way of the ideals she pursued. She would go to the very end of her mission.

• • •

Hardly had Fary returned from her trip when she again had to take the way to Mboupbène. Her mother had fallen ill and was calling Fary to her side.

As tiny as a child, completely changed, Lala's emaciated body disappeared in the middle of the bed under a heap of blankets covering her soaking wet body. Healers had been called in from everywhere and were busying themselves at her bedside. They mixed brews, powders, and roots that were rejected as soon as they had passed Lala's lips.

Mayacine was desolate. He could not bear losing his faithful companion. The children were lamenting. For the second time Fary took over the household.

• • •

"Fary, Fary," murmured her mother, leaning on her elbow, "here you are at last! I am thirsty."

Fary ran toward the fountain and brought back a pot of water. Holding her mother's head with one hand, she made her drink first water, then some gruel. A miracle. Lala did not vomit. Fary called her father, whispering in his ear.

The room was emptied of people. At present Fary was alone with her mother. She relieved Lala of her numerous blankets, changed her damp clothing which clung to her body, and aired out the room where the sun had not been allowed for a long time.

"What hurts you, mother?"

"Nothing hurts me, daughter. I only feel so tired that at times I can't even speak. It has been thus since the day after you left. Once again in my dream I saw myself thrown in the hollow trunk of the baobab tree.

"Fary, I have often been sick. Previously, the seriousness of my condition worried me, but I always had hopes of recovering. This time it is quite different; I have an incurable illness. Sooner or later I will die of it.

"Small signs, insignificant for ordinary mortals, have become significant to me. Dreams and a lot of premonitions announce the end I am afraid of. Yes, daughter, I am afraid, afraid to die.

"The mystery of the great beyond terrifies me. This hole, which long ago made you tremble and made you ill, obsesses me. I would not want to be buried there. Never. Do you hear me? Never! My soul will not find peace unless my body is buried in a tomb. I have an intuition that only the earth can prepare me for the mysteries beyond the grave.

"Since your marriage I have nurtured a secret hope. Thanks to you, many things have changed for the better. But the most difficult problem remains, the law that decrees that our bodies must be buried in tree trunks. Try to intercede with your husband for him to grant us the right to have a cemetery as our tradition demands.

"*Gouye Guéol* should be completely destroyed. Nothing should be left for future generations of this degrading monument to the past. It surely would be profanation, but in my opinion it would be less serious than the eternal presence of these graves, symbols of paganism on the soil of Mboupbène. You can do it, Fary, I am convinced of it. A woman can get anything from the man who loves her."

"Be without fear, mother, regain your strength and get well." She forced herself to make her voice sound clear and reassuring even though revolt made her blood boil and her veins swell. She was close to tears, but her awareness of the new task she must face was a source of strength guiding her attitude and her words.

"I am grateful to you for everything. What I am today is only the fruit of your efforts, your patience, your generosity, and the sacrifices you have always made.

"Don't be misled by my youth. I have always observed you, admired you. I saw how you lived. I saw you suffer or be silent when faced with arrogance, injustice, and insults. My appearing to be an innocent child was only to make your troubles easier to bear, not to give you more.

"You must not die. I need you. I need your love and your wisdom. My father, my brothers and sisters also need you. We will have it, our cemetery, as our religion ordains.

"*Gouye Guéol* will not engulf your body. I think I already promised you that a long time ago. Don't you remember? I renew my commitment to you. I swear by all that is dearest to me that this cemetery will be destroyed."

• • •

Slowly, as if by a miracle, the sick woman became stronger. She asked Fary about her life in Tiali.

"How is everything going for you?"

"Thank God I have followed your advice. Coura and Mayoro are my faithful friends. The queen mother has become my ally. I managed to get her to rally to our cause. A little later we must see your weavers to order the *pagnes* and the *boubous* I want to give her. Frequent presents have established good relations with my husband's family. I have to order a new wardrobe. Friendship is expensive in Tiali."

"And Bocar?"

"I accept him, mother, since such was your command, yours and my father's. For humility and politeness, you have been my example. I try to satisfy his every desire. But, unlike you, I don't always say 'yes'. From time to time he must find some reticence."

"I don't agree and surely your father wouldn't. You sound like Sokhna. She is quite nice, but very independent. Don't listen too much to her talk about women's emancipation. She all too often forgets the example of your great-great-grandmother. Follow my example. Be humble. Accept the *pagne* and let Bocar wear the pants."

Fary promised. "What news of my brothers and sisters? I am anxious to see them."

"You are more likely to see Biram for it is almost impossible to get hold of Tior. He is always mischievous, lazy, and without shame. He does not take after either of us. He has not changed one iota in spite of my good advice and your father's remonstrances.

"Not a day goes by without one of the neighbors coming in with a complaint on her lips. He steals chickens, plunders the fields, chases the girls, and is insolent to his elders. He worries me. I really despair of seeing him change. If he hasn't changed at an age where he wears your father's shoes, he never will."

"Mother, I don't think Tior's case is as hopeless as you think. His impertinence is the result of incomprehension. Please forgive me for it is not for me, your daughter, to tell you what to do, but it is only because of our conversation that I dare speak to you in this way. You and my father have always shown a marked preference for Biram while Tior received endless recriminations. Jealous of this partiality, he only reacted by increasing his jokes and his mischievousness."

"You could not have said it better, daughter. He is so jealous of Biram that he pretends he also wants to get married, even though he is still a snotnose, just because your brother plans to get married soon."

Fary could not help laughing out loud. Her mother continued, "Try to talk to him. You are the only one he listens to. This child brings me so much shame and creates so many worries for me that sometimes I think I will die on the spot."

"It's a promise, mother. I will speak to him as to the adult he believes he is. But from now on you should consider his feelings and treat him like a man.

"When is Biram getting married, Mother?"

"Have you seen Mayoro?"

"About what?"

"About a message I had given him for you concerning this marriage."

"No, mother, I haven't. He is very busy preparing his marriage to Sokhna."

"We had a lot of surprises and difficulties with the parents of Biram's fiancée. Maye is your first cousin, your uncle's daughter, so it's all in the family. I can swear that I promoted this union because the girl seduced me. She impressed me by her charm and her good manners. Unfortunately, I can't say the same for her mother. All I was afraid of on her account has happened. She has shown limitless ambition, exacting a dowry which has never been heard of in Mboupbène, and all because of you.

" 'When one has a princess for a sister, one can afford anything,' Maye's mother said, and her words came right back to me. Some good souls, so-called friends of your aunt told me."

"I am not surprised, mother. Meanness, jealousy, and slander first take hold in ones closest to you before they spread to others.

"Never fear. I have a personal fortune large enough to provide a dowry for all my brothers and sisters. I will double the sum and the goods my aunt is asking for. They may sneer at the princess, but the princess will rise to the occasion."

A happy smile made Lala's eyes come alive. She was proud of her daughter's worthy ambition.

● ● ●

Their conversation was often interrupted by the coming and going of Modou, Fary's youngest brother, who was in his twelfth year. Timid and uncommunicative, he loved his mother with a possessive, unhealthy love, following her everywhere like a shadow.

"Lala," Mayacine used to say, "cut the apron strings of that boy, set him free, you will make a woman of him. At his age he should spend more time with me or boys his own age."

Modou, his head bent, shot smoldering glances at his father. He hated him with a passion ever since Mayacine had left their sick mother in favor of Astou, his latest wife. The oath that he would protect his mother made the child accomplish many things in spite of his youth.

While Yaram and Yandé, lazy and scatterbrained, took advantage of Lala's illness to flee from the household chores, Modou split wood, filled the water basins, tended the fire and secretly washed his mother's clothes. The impertinent Yandé, in her conversations with Yaram, never stopped teasing him. "Have you ever seen anything like it, sister?"

"Like what, Yaram?"

"Such an attachment for his mother. It's a sickness. A very serious sickness for which we must find a remedy as quickly as possible."

Modou split his wood with fury.

"Bintou might be the remedy. Our little cousin is not without interest to you know who, who ogles her when he is not in his mother's wake."

"Leave me in peace, you two," Modou yelled, running towards his sisters, the ax held high. "I don't love anybody. I'll never get married. I have my mother. She is the gentlest, the prettiest of all women. That's enough for me. I will protect her. Whoever will hurt one hair of her head will have his head split like this wood." With one thrust he split the log.

● ● ●

Fary was going into the yard when she found herself face-to-face with Yaram, who, true to her habits, had been listening behind the door. She had grown into a young girl of remarkable beauty. She was tall and slim with an upturned nose and lively, mocking eyes. A perpetual smile gave her face a mischievous expression.

"Will you never change? At your age you should be dyeing, hairdressing, or embroidering rather than spending your time listening and spreading gossip. For who listens behind doors also gossips."

Yaram hung her head sullenly.

"Next time I catch you I'll box your ears."

For the first time in her life Yaram dared to answer back to her sister, "The people are right. You have changed. Your title of princess made you blow up like a balloon. There is really no reason for it. I'd rather die than marry a dwarf."

Fary advanced slowly on her, ready to slap her. Yaram ran off as fast as a hare.

● ● ●

The fat Yandé, also being true to herself, was scraping the bottom of the pot. The kitchen was her domain. She chewed noisily on the crust which stuck halfway out of her mouth. Not one crumb of it fell to the floor for an experienced tongue quick as a serpent caught it. She smiled at her sister as she went up to her, wiping her greasy hands on her *pagne*.

"Fary, I would like to come to Tiali with you. I have already asked our father's permission several times, but he always refuses. Biram and Tior never stop talking about the riches of the palace, especially the feast in your honor when you delivered the sheep. Is it all true?"

"It is true, Yandé."

The child's eyes shone. She hopped up and down on her short legs, her fat belly jiggling.

"Take me with you. I'll work. I'll be docile. I'll do anything you want."

"I will take you, but under one condition. Try to lose weight. If not, the people at the palace will make fun of you."

Yandé suppressed a sob. Tears ran down her face. Fary felt sorry for her and regretted her words. She was about to comfort her sister when Yandé looked daggers at her and said, "Are they also making fun of your husband, the dwarf?"

Yandé, who had always been timid and afraid, had backed up. Disrespectful, hands on her hips, she stood before Fary, defying her with unequalled impertinence.

"What's gotten into both of you? A few minutes ago Yaram, now you. Stupid little girl. Since when dare you speak to me like that? Are you forgetting that I am your elder, that I have fed you, washed you, dried you, wiped your nose? Are you forgetting that you owe me respect? Are you forgetting . . . ?"

Yandé cut her off. "Why should I pay eternal tribute to you, Fary? *Li wone, woni na,* the past is over. The whip, the insults, the orders, all that is finished. The absurd Yandé, Yandé the clod, Yandé the docile one, always being lectured to about mere trifles.

"Yandé, the clumsy one, is no longer your slave. Just dare lay a hand on me and you shall see." Aggressively, she advanced towards Fary, her back arched, her belly out like a pregnant woman at the end of her term.

"You have made your life hell. With less ambition, I'll make mine paradise."

Fary remained speechless. She was terribly shaken by her

sister's conduct, but especially by the painful truth which had been spoken for the first time. "You have made your life hell." Yes, and what hell! Cruel truth, undeniable truth which only confirmed Coura's bitter words.

• • •

Fary had become Princess Fary Mayacine Mboup, who overshadowed all other women through her charm, her elegance, and her generosity. Her name had become known in all the fiefs of the principality and even across the borders.

Sometimes she helped her husband resolve thorny problems, assuming the role of a lawyer in developing new laws which were all to the advantage of her race and the condition of women. Her diplomacy was of great help to Bocar. Thanks to her shrewd insight, enemies slowly rallied to the regime. She nevertheless remained discreet, and gave the impression that she lived only for her son and her household.

Her co-wives tirelessly ran from *marabout* to *marabout*, convinced that some day they would get rid of Fary.

Bocar's daughters, incensed by their father's attitude, revenged the outrage by attacking Fary relentlessly. Lies, insults, and plots were daily occurrences. They had no effect on the princess, who was safe in the love of her husband.

Mayoro, the faithful *beuk-nek,* was now the great steward of the palace. His new station allowed him to realize his old dream: Sokhna finally became his wife.

• • •

Fary was confined a second time for twins, identical twins, as alike as two drops of water, two Bocar Djiwan Malicks in miniature. Coura's prediction had come true. With courage and determination Fary accepted this new misfortune.

On this particular day it had been raining incessantly since dawn. Fary filled the *anda,* the incense burner, with glowing cinders and perfumed the room. She prepared hot water and clean, scented *pagnes* for her husband.

Bocar, after a succulent meal, stretched out and soaked his feet in the basin of water. Fary washed them, dried them, and massaged them, a delicate ritual into which Sokhna had initiated her. She helped him undress, then took her own clothes off, and stretched out beside him. She was trembling.

"What is it, Fary?" Bocar asked her, putting his little arms around her. "Your body feels hot. You are shivering. Are you ill?"

"It's nothing, uncle. I only have a headache. I often get them when it is raining and it has not stopped since this morning. Don't be anxious about me, you have enough worries with your government. I don't want to be yet another source of worry for you."

"You are just as important to me as my government. You are the most precious thing I have in the world."

He rose to fetch a vial from his bag and poured black liquid into a bowl, made her swallow a few mouthfuls, and poured the rest over her head.

● ● ●

The next morning Fary was the same. She nevertheless saw to her duties. The prince summoned a fetishist, who after spending the night in the palace, had incense burned to chase the evil eye and the evil working against Fary which caused her illness.

The next morning Fary could not get up. She was afflicted with a persistent headache that defied all remedies. Her co-wives, who had been told by their spies, saw a helping hand from destiny. They again dared hope and took courage.

"You see, Yande, I was right to counsel patience. The 'untouchable' is sick. Tierno has assured us that she would not get up from her sickbed again."

"In that case, it is all over for her and I think this is the second prediction coming true. The princess doesn't stop yelling. She is going mad, stark raving mad. I will go to any length to get rid of her. I will stop at nothing."

"The *marabout* should give us another *gris-gris* to bury in the courtyard. We were to bring him the hoof of a donkey. Did you see to it as I asked?"

"No, Falla, I was not able to."

"And why not?"

"I could not get it because it is the prince's uncle who supervises not only the treasury, but also the slaughterhouse and the livestock. He knows everything that goes on here. The stable boy, whom I had asked secretly, went and told the old lecher, who now has asked to see me. And do you know what he proposed as an exchange?"

"I can guess, but leave him to me. He will see. I will get it, this hoof."

Yande's eyes widened and she asked, "And just how do you expect to get it?"

"That's my business. Find a good reason to be absent and let's meet tomorrow after the second prayer of the day at the road out of Tiali."

• • •

During the following night Fary was particularly agitated. She threw off all the sheets that covered her. She was delirious. Her eyes wide open, she stared at Bocar. She yelled like a demented woman.

"No, they will take me. They are calling me. Stop them, Prince. They are going toward the tree, in the hole. I don't want to. I don't want to die." She fell into unconsciousness.

"What tree is she talking about?" Bocar asked the fetishist.

"Surely about the haunted tree at the exit of Tiali, where the *djins*, the spirits meet at night."

Fary was given such a strong dose of incense that she fainted in her husband's arms.

Her condition worsened the next day. She clung to Bocar, clawed at him, tore his clothes, and shouted like a madwoman.

"No, not the tree, it will swallow me! The children, too. Destroy it, Prince, destroy it. It is the only way to save us. The funeral tree at Mboupbène." She again fell unconscious and could be revived only with difficulty.

The prince of Tiali, his head in his hands, was despair itself. He turned to his wife asking, "What are you saying, Fary?"

"Destroy the cemetery of Mboupbène."

Once again the tom-toms were heard. The wise men, the soothsayers, the fetishists, and the *marabouts* were being summoned by the prince. They were to live at the palace and prove their knowledge by finding a cure for the princess other than the destruction of the funeral trees of Mboupbène. After a delay of three days they gave their answer.

The wise men of Ndouli came first. Resting in her bed, her body covered with a mutitude of *pagnes*, Fary seemed to be asleep. From time to time a low moan rose from her lips. The wise men were speaking in low voices.

"What did you see, Amary?"

"A panther who appeared at each of my incantations. And you Mody?"

"A serpent around a tree in *Gouye Guéol* whose mouth swallowed everyone who came near the tree."

"You see, brother, the spirits are against the destruction of the cemetery. They appeared to both of us in different forms, but their meaning was the same."

"What are we to tell the prince? He is very upset by his wife's illness. We have to consider his feelings. Let us act in a way that will not disappoint him and preserve his good opinion of us."

"We will tell him separately and in different words that the spirits ask for a time span of three Fridays to give an answer. In the meantime, he should give something white to the poor, milk, a hen, a sheep, or a *pagne*. By then we shall see how the illness goes and take other steps."

The soothsayers from Tatane followed. Bocar allowed them some minutes alone in Fary's room as he had done for their predecessors.

"Sorry, I spent a terrible night, the longest in my existence. I don't know how you feel about it, but I wash my hands of the illness of this *griotte*. All night long I was beaten by the cursed spirits of Mboupbène. To touch those trees is like a death warrant. I don't want to risk it."

"My meditation last night showed me an extraordinary sight. Violent thunder and lightning coming from a sky as black as the shadows fell on the whole earth except on the baobabs of *Gouye Guéol*."

"Misfortune will befall all of us if only one of us touches a leaf of those trees. Let us suggest sacrifices to the prince. If they don't cure his wife's illness, they will make it less severe."

"What, for example?"

"Let him shed the blood of seven four-legged animals, goat, sheep, or beef, and share the meat among seven different families who each have three boys and four girls."

When the fetishist came in, Fary's throat was rattling.

"Mayecor, on my father's belt, I refuse to treat the Princess Fary Mboup. My life depends on it. The spirits pelted me with stones all night long."

"I am trembling for my own life, Fara. A lion stretched out under these cursed trees threatened me with his claws and his fangs all night long."

"What to do?"

"Tell the prince to bathe his wife for seven days with water from seven wells coming from seven different villages. I have heard it said a long time ago by my ancestors that these baths chase evil spirits."

"What do you say, Serigne Mor?"

"Khadam, I had trouble receiving clear *bistikhar*. For the first time in my life I am confronted with such problems. The omens are bad. All night long I have been attacked by all sorts of monsters."

"Let's leave these trees alone. They have existed since the time of our most remote ancestors. They were haunted even before this cemetery existed. Bocar has brought his misfortunes upon himself. Let him suffer the consequences."

"I believe you are right. To attack these powers so much stronger than we would be suicide. As for me, I never once could get hold of the *rawane*, the spirit. It escaped me every time."

"Mark down a *gris-gris* for the head, a *safara* for three baths on three successive Thursdays. Recommend also the sacrifice of a white hen. I will prescribe a *gris-gris* for the kidneys. I will ask for seven bowls of *lakh*, porridge, to be given to the poor on Monday, as well as the sacrifice of a red hen spotted with black like the fruit of the palm tree."

● ● ●

The prince of Tiali applied the various treatments to the letter. None was effective. Fary went from bad to worse. Her heartbreaking moans tortured her husband day and night. He was terribly afraid for her.

Tiali's finances melted like sugar in water. The bills were exorbitant. The prince made the *marabouts* come from all over the hills and through the valleys to look for whoever could cure his wife without destroying the cemetery of Mboupbène.

Surely he did love her. She had become the most precious thing on earth for him. He had proved his love for her many times by granting all the privileges asked by her people. Had he not gone beyond that? Had he not killed to assert his authority and install his wife's relatives in his government? But to destroy *Gouye Guêol*? He was afraid. Afraid of the spirits of his ancestors. Despite the rigors of his new religion, he could not free himself of these pagan traditions rooted in him for such a long time. He had abandoned them; no sacrifices, no pagan rituals since his conversion.

The spirits don't forgive such neglect and they had, of course, to be consulted before embarking on such an enterprise.

He decided to go and see old Gane, the keeper of the cultural heritage of the prince's family. After isolating herself in the sanctuary for a few minutes, she gave a categorical refusal to the prince.

"Your ancestors are opposed. They formally forbid you to touch these baobabs. If you touch just one of them, lightning will strike you, your family, and the entire country."

• • •

On that day, Mayoro, full of concern, asked how Fary was.

"My prince, how is your wife?"

"Very poorly."

"Has there been no improvement since her last treatments?"

"None."

"I can't understand that. Never to my knowledge have so many wise men been gathered at the bedside of one person."

"She continues to be delirious and asking me to destroy *Gouye Guéol.*"

"Then why not do it? The remains of the deceased could be buried afterwards. To tell you the truth, I can see no other solution if this course of action is the only thing that will make her well."

"She is asking me to burn *Gouye Guéol!*"

"*Asbomrah lahil,* what profanation, what infamy. Burning the dead. Never, never would your subjects forgive you."

"Oh Mayoro, what a dilemma! What do you advise me to do, my faithful friend?"

"I will go and see my man, the one who helped us make your marriage possible."

"Go to see him, he is my last resort."

• • •

The *marabout* arrived surrounded by the greatest secrecy and quietly entered the room of the sick princess, whose strident cries tore the silence of the night. He was unrecognizable. He wore a large turban that covered his head and face like a Tuareg. He was accompanied by a boy about fifteen years old who carried a large goatskin pouch on his head.

After the customary greeting, the *marabout* had the room cleared and remained alone with the patient. After long hours of being alone with Fary, he asked for an isolated room in the palace where he could meditate for seven days and seven nights.

• • •

Prince Bocar now was only a shadow of his former self. He was as thin as a skeleton. His eyes, bulging more than ever in his enormous head, made him a terrifying spectacle. Even now Fary could not repress the instinctive revulsion she felt when his hands lovingly caressed her forehead bathed in perspiration. Despite all of Bocar's love and generosity, Fary could never overcome her loathing. Her body submitted to the man, her husband, but her heart could never welcome him. His touch always evoked the same shivers of disgust, the same bitter taste in her mouth, the same cold perspiration. There was no remedy for it.

• • •

After seven days and seven nights of *khalwa*, of being isolated with the spirits, Tierno had a long meeting with the prince. His conclusion was that *Gouye Guéol* should be destroyed by fire. On this point he was definite. Emphatically, more eloquent than ever, he spoke to the prince, "Seven white sheep and seven red bulls will be sacrificed and their meat distributed in the village. Bowls of millet mush and soured milk will be shared among the families. Then you will burn the trees. The spirit which tortures the princess and causes her terrible illness is hiding in one of the numerous tree trunks. The fire must be lit from logs coming from the baobabs at the four corners of Mboupbène, east, west, north and south, in the night from Thursday to Friday.

"After that you will build a cemetery according to the tradition with graves dug in the earth. You will face serious problems, Prince Bocar Djiwan Malick. Your life will be in danger. Your subjects will be angry with you, some because of the new cemetery, others because of the profanation by fire. But most important to you is your wife's life.

"Do not forget the help I have given you and will continue to give to you as long as you need it. As long as I live you can count on my knowledge."

The prince did not give his answer right away. He gave himself three days for reflection, during which the illness became worse. Day and night the palace rang with the cries of his wife, who had become hysterical. At last he gave in.

• • •

The destruction of the cemetery of Mboupbène was at the origin of fratricidal fighting without precedent in the country's history. Three attempts were made on Bocar's life and failed. Fary's children several times barely escaped kidnapping and were saved only through the vigilence and faithfulness of Coura and Mayoro.

The enemies were now countless. For all of Tiali the destruction of the cemetery was the work of the *griotte*. Secretly, intrigues were spun against the cursed woman who undeniably was the source of all calamities which would now befall the country.

As revenge, Mboupbène was attacked. Houses were destroyed, harvests burned. Fary's parents barely escaped the carnage. They had been a prime target for the furious mob.

Destroying the cemetery was a desperate act, but it was the salvation of Fary.

Three months after her second confinement, Fary once again took the road for Mboupbène to undergo the rites of protection. Her family received her joyfully. Yaram's and Yandé's scorn which she had experienced during her first visit was now forgotten. At present they were full of love for their elder sister.

Her mother's state of health was the only shadow falling on Fary's happiness. Sickness had wasted Lala. She had changed even more. Suddenly aged, even the slightest effort exhausted her. All her strength was now devoted to prayer. The smiles of the newborn infants brought joy to her lined and worried face.

One morning she could not rise from her bed. She called her daughter and in a barely audible voice told her, "Fary, take this money and go pay the shoemaker, the weaver, and the basketmaker. They will tell you what I owe them. You will see to it that your aunt in Tatane gets these jewels. I wanted her daughter to have them for her wedding."

"What is the matter, mother?" Fary asked anxiously. "Why do you act as if I were to carry out your last wishes?"

"You are carrying them out, daughter. Don't be afraid, come here, give me your hand. I bless you, I ask your forgiveness. I have no illusions. I am going to die, I know it. The reprieve is over. On my deathbed I ask the Lord to grant you long life, good health, and a happy marriage. May your children grow up in peace and happiness and help you before you get tired.

"Thanks to you I was able to devote my last hours to God without being haunted by those terrifying baobabs. I will die in peace knowing that my body will be buried as it is prescribed by the Holy Scriptures.

"Now nurse your son and call your father to me. I bless you. My eternal blessing I bestow on you."

A few moments later her father come out of Lala's room in tears. Her mother had just died.

A messenger was dispatched to Tiali. The prince soon arrived accompanied by a large escort.

• • •

The funeral of Lala Mboup, the mother-in-law of Prince Bocar Djiwan Malick, attracted a large crowd such as had never before been assembled on the soil of Mboupbène.

The body of the deceased, wrapped in a white shroud, was laid in the grave, a rectangular trench disappearing little by little under shovelfuls of sand.

After a last prayer, the men dispersed. They left the cemetery as if the devil were at their heels. When the people who had accompanied the deceased to her last resting place were leaving, the superstition was that the deceased woke up with the name of his relatives and closest friends on his lips. The most grieving friend and the most helpful relative were the first to flee the cemetery for fear of hearing themselves called by the deceased. Several times the gravedigger had picked up shoes, bonnets, prayerbeads, or other things lost during the flight of the crowds after the funeral.

The Imam, who had directed the funeral services, had gathered all the people present to thank them and tell them that all ceremonies pertaining to the funeral were over now. He asked them to leave and suspend all activities which would go against Islamic custom.

The relatives from Mboupbène, Tiali, Ndame Ndouli, and Tatane went home.

• • •

Once the Imam had left, a crowd of women poured into Mboupbène. The queen mother was leading them. She had her son called to her and said, "Son, I agree with the Imam concerning moderation, contemplation, and the respect which must be observed at a funeral. A funeral is neither a baptism nor a wedding, but don't forget that Lala Mboup was the mother-in-law of the Prince of Tiali and her funeral could never be the same as any other.

"I don't want to contradict the Imam, but there are exceptions to everything. Look at the fingers of the hand, they are not alike. These differences also exist in our society.

"You will order the sacrifice of seven bulls, one for each day of the seven days we will be here. Bags of millet will be pounded and made into cous-cous, a mush to feed our hosts. You will also give me money, a large sum, which will be distributed among the family."

The prince had to obey his mother, even though his whole being rebelled against such practices.

• • •

Her eyes vacant, Fary responded in a forced manner to the people's expressions of sympathy. Their commiserations were lacking sincerity. The people were famished by successive years of drought and had come to stuff themselves with beef liver, rib steaks, tenderloin, and round steak. Men, women, and children became freeloaders whose arms were heavy with poorly wrapped parcels which left traces of blood on the woven mats. Fary had to smile when she responded to the condolences offered by Aby, her brother's mother-in-law, whose meat parcel, cleverly tied and carried on her head, was leaking blood on her back where a spot of red became bigger and bigger.

Fary had to smile when old Daour expressed his sympathy. An enormous lump, undoubtedly a hunk of meat, made his pocket bulge and his chest appear asymmetric. She was still smiling when Fatuna, the gossip, came up to her pressing a bundle, unquestionably of meat, against her hip.

She smiled at the complexity of man. She was caught entirely in the throes of grief. These people were caught entirely by hunger. What sincerity in disguise! She was maturing. She was beginning to understand human nature.

"*Siguil ndigale,* my condolences."

"*Siguil sa wala,*" Fary answered mechanically.

She saw herself as she was a long time ago when, accompanied by Coura, she had witnessed the funeral which was to decide her fate.

She heard Sokhna's voice, "Yes, you will be a princess. People will prostrate themselves at your feet." She remembered Coura's words then, "*Daga goumou diam,* never will you cut the bonds of slavery." She was a woman, almost a child, with empty hands confronting centuries of tradition which since the beginning of time existed as does the sky, immutable above our heads. "No, Fary, you will never succeed. Marry Gana. You love him. He is beautiful and your children will be as beautiful as angels."

Her children were not angels, but monsters. Monsters like their father. She still hated him. She would never be able to love him. She would suffer him. She would get him to make still more concessions to help her people. She would squeeze him like a lemon. She would take everything from him to rehabilitate her people.

As the tears, drop by drop, rolled down her cheeks, the young village girls, *pagnes* in hand, were fanning her. Their pure voices rose in a melodious chant now famous in Mboupbène during family ceremonies where this chant held a place of honor:

Fary Mayacine Mboup,
Fary, our princess, dry your tears.
Our hearts on this day of sadness
grieve with yours.
To mourn our dear mother with you,
Lala, blessed woman, chosen among women.
Dry your tears, beloved sister,
do not grieve.
You who have cut the bonds of slavery
You, thanks to whom we walk
our heads held high,
Open your eyes. Look,
we walk at your side.
Your way is the way of honor.
Your tears are our tears
and your grief our grief.
With our forces united and our hearts humble
we kiss your feet and await your command.
Command, Fary, Princess, command.
Our forehead to the ground, we will kiss
your feet.

THE END

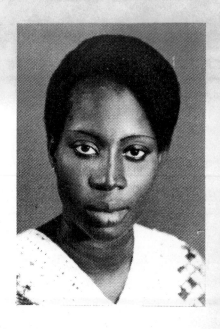

Nafissatou Diallo (1941-1982), a well-respected Senegalese author, won an award from the International Association of French Language Speakers for her first novel, *De Tilène au Plateau: Une Enfance Dakaroise* (translated into English under the title *A Dakar Childhood*). It is an autobiographical novel, which describes her father and grandfather, and was written as a testimonial to a way of life that had ended. Two other novels, *Le Fort Maudit* and *Awa, La Petite Senegalaise*, also describe the traditional and modern aspects of Senegalese society. Madame Diallo took an active part in the social services of her country as midwife and director of a maternal and child health care center on the outskirts of Dakar.

Ann Woollcombe holds a diploma from the Institut Catholique in Paris and spent four years working in Cameroon, where she developed a keen interest in African literature. She has travelled in Senegal, Morocco and Indonesia, and now lives in Canada with her husband and daughter. She is currently working on a translation of Brick Oussaid's *Les Coquelicots de L'Oriental: Chronique d'une Famille Berbere Marocaine* (to be published by Three Continents Press as *Poppy Pickers: Chronicle of a Berber Family*).

Barbara H. Scherer is a professional writer in Washington, D.C. with an interest in anthropology and linguistics.